Sophie's Path

A Branching Narrative Romance

By Fleur Blüm

First edition 27 May, 2018

Copyright © 2018 Fleur Blüm
ISBN 978-0648365402

Editor: Annie Seaton
Cover Design: GetCovers

Published by Fleur Blüm, Melbourne, Australia

Start

You wake up to the sound of your alarm. It's loud and grating and you hate the noise, but if you didn't you would never get up. You hit snooze, although you know it only delays the pain of getting out of the warm, cosy embrace of the bed.

With a groan you flip back the covers and shiver when the cold air touches your skin. You pull on your dressing gown and shuffle out to the kitchen, where you click on the coffee machine and plop two slices of grainy bread into the toaster. You've been telling yourself for some time that the grainier the bread, the better it is for you even though you don't like the texture.

You stare off into space, leaning back on the counter while your coffee dribbles into the cup. You consider the day ahead; office gossip in the morning followed by perfunctory emailing, then a department meeting in which you, along with everyone else, will try to keep the boredom from your face.

You hear the click and pop that says the toast is ready. The aroma of coffee starts to waken your senses.

Only about half the office staff is there when you arrive a little before your usual start time of eight-thirty.

You turn on your computer and start to look over your emails.

"She's always late," says a quiet voice over your shoulder. You know that soft, gravelly voice without turning around, it's Max. Emily's desk is still unoccupied.

"You're right, but what can you do about it? She's not one of yours, she's in Finance, so her lateness is outside of your domain," you say as you turn to face him. His silvery hair is impeccable as usual and his lined face lit with a sly grin.

The two of you have developed a habit of complaining about the comings and goings of the staff, and Emily in particular. You've maintained a close relationship with Max since transferring out of his department and into Client Services not long ago. He can get away with more now he's no longer your direct supervisor and you've been able to get more out of his advice when you're not trying to juggle your needs with the needs of the department.

The people who arrive late change from day to day, with reasons offered varying from traffic and train delays, to flexible working hours and meetings out of the office. Except for Emily, who seems to have her own schedule, whether it's coming in to work on time, or getting reports in. It frustrates you, because you are someone who gets satisfaction from a job done well, and on time. But as you said to Max, she doesn't work for your department.

Emily comes in about ten with Lola trailing behind her. You've never understood exactly what Lola gets out of the relationship. You've had a couple of pleasant interactions with her, but her closeness with Emily has made you wary of getting too friendly. A little nugget of guilt forms in your belly as you watch the pair of them instead of getting on with your work.

As the staff meeting approaches, always before lunch on a Wednesday, the worst possible time in your opinion, your boss, Candace, asks you to pass on her apologies and hands you a report.

"Can you present this to the meeting? It's just those sales figures that Aubrey asked for last week. I've got to go meet the rep from Telstra. You're a star, Soph!" She flicks her long ponytail over her shoulder as she walks off, leaving you no time to ask questions.

You open the report and look over the charts; it's not good news. "That's why she arranged to be in a meeting this week," you mutter to yourself.

Even though she's thrown you in the deep end you can't stay mad at Candace. She's still new and trying to pick up the pieces left behind by her predecessor. Despite his occasional fire-breathing, Aubrey, the owner, runs the company more like a family than a business.

Are we still on for lunch today, babe? Felicity's text message arrives while you're in the meeting.

I gotta get through a presentation first. I'll let you know.

You know your response will annoy Felicity so close to lunchtime, but you know you won't be able to go out for lunch if the presentation goes sideways.

"Where is Candace? She was going to give us the sales report." Aubrey asks, his wide nostrils flared. You try not to flinch at his thunderous voice; he always sounds angry even when he isn't.

"She had to meet with Telstra, I have the figures here," you say as you start to pass around the charts. Aubrey merely nods.

The presentation is difficult, the results aren't great and the charts are somewhat complicated to explain to staff outside your team. You have to field a few curly questions from Aubrey and the other managers, but you're relieved that you don't completely screw it up.

When you came into the meeting Emily and Calvin, from Payroll, are sitting side by side. At first you thought they might have been continuing something from before the meeting but when you look over after your presentation is finished, and Emily is smiling and patting Calvin's arm.

Just because I don't like her, doesn't mean she's up to something, you think and try to put it from your mind.

The meeting doesn't finish until after one and you're ravenous. Everyone scatters quickly and you start to text Felicity. Emily and Calvin go into Calvin's office and close the door.

CHOOSE:

If you cancel with Felicity and eat at your desk to see what happens, go to <u>p 7.</u>

If you ignore them and go out to lunch go to <u>p 148.</u>

C1 O1 You chose to cancel with Felicity and eat at your desk to see what happens with Calvin and Emily …

Sorry, the meeting didn't go as well as I wanted. I need to stay in the office to keep an eye on something. Rain check for tomoz? you text Felicity. You're not being entirely truthful with her, but it's not something you want to discuss in a text.

You pull out the can of soup that you have in a bottom desk drawer for days when you can't get out. Calvin's office is on the way to the kitchen but you don't hear anything from behind the closed door as you pass. You regret putting off your best friend to spy on Emily, it seems petty now.

You put your soup into a bowl and set it in the microwave.

"Thanks for taking that presentation for me, Sophie," Candace says as she sweeps into the kitchen, back from her meeting.

"Jackie, from Telstra, really needed to meet before she went up to Sydney for a conference and it was the only time she could swing it," she continues.

It sounds true given what you know about your boss and about Telstra. You've fielded questions from Jackie before and she is often strapped for time.

"Aubrey thinks you were avoiding him," you say as you take your soup from the microwave. You're so hungry the smell of the heavily processed minestrone makes your mouth water. "I know I would if I were him."

"I did tell him, perhaps he forgot. Anyway I've got a meeting with him later, I can beg forgiveness in person. He knows how Telstra can be and the figures weren't great, but they weren't bad enough that I was throwing you under the bus."

Still standing at the kitchen bench, you take a spoonful of soup, allowing the silence to sit between you.

"Well, I can see you're on your lunchbreak so I'll leave you to it, find me when you're done and we can debrief." Candace smiles, the full force of her very straight, very white teeth washes over you. You aren't really mad at her; it's your belly doing all the talking, so you sit down and demolish the soup before continuing the conversation.

After you've eaten, you head over to Candace's office. She's on the phone, but waves you into the guest chair in front of her.

"Close the door," she mouths, still on the phone.

You close the door and take a seat, trying not to listen to the conversation.

"Yeah, definitely, it needs to be done ASAP, the longer we leave it the more it'll fester. I'll put my best person on it." She nods and makes agreeing noises for a little while longer, then ends the call.

Candace's face is serious; her lips are compressed into a line and her very white teeth are no longer visible.

"That was Jeremy Read. He's the executive assistant to the CEO of a software development company we've just taken on. They've been dealing with Jason, but he's new and hasn't been handling them very well. Jeremy is a contact of mine from way back, he's how we got the contract in the first place, so he came to me to say that the CEO is ready to drop us." Candace pulls her hair forward over her shoulder and starts to play with it without seeming to be aware of what she's doing.

"I need you to take over, show them some love, go to their office and get as much out of Jeremy as you can and repair the damage."

"Right." You were expecting to give Candace a rundown of the meeting and she's blindsided you with this new project.

"This takes priority over everything else you have on. I'll email you everything we have on them, contracts and correspondence and the rest of it." She pauses, and exhales a long breath.

"Thanks for taking that meeting for me, as I said it more important to make sure Telstra was happy than Aubrey. We can't afford to lose another big client right now. How did it go?"

You run her through the meeting, you don't mention Emily and Calvin whispering or the closed door meeting. It's probably nothing, and mentioning it would feel foolish.

"Sounds like you handled that really well. I knew you could." Candace looks down at her fingernails, they're short and jagged, and the skin around the cuticles is red as though she's been biting them. "Are you able to visit

Jeremy this afternoon? You won't have time to go over the emails, but I think it would be better if they see a new Drake and Co. face sooner rather than later. Jason really dropped the ball, not his fault of course, I should have been supporting him, but we're in damage control mode now and you're the best I have for building good relationships quickly."

"Uh, let me have a look at the calendar," you say. You check the afternoon's meetings on your phone, taking a moment to consider the change in priorities. "Where's the office?"

"Prahran."

You have a four o'clock with another client back in the city, and it's nearly two now. It will be tight, but if Candace really needs it, you can squeeze it in.

CHOOSE:

If you choose to do a short meet and greet with the client, go to <u>p 11.</u>

If you push the meeting to tomorrow, go to <u>p 80.</u>

C1.1 O1 You chose to squeeze in a short meet and greet…

You do a quick calculation in your head. "I guess if I cab over there I can spend an hour or so showing my face, but I have to be back here by four…"

"That's great news, I appreciate it." Candace seems relieved, her smile is almost back to her usual brightness as you leave her office.

You gather up your laptop and the spiral notebook you take everywhere before heading downstairs to hail a taxi. As you struggle to get into the back of the taxi with your arms full, Calvin and Emily walk out of the building together.

Emily looks around briefly before taking both his hands in hers and leans over to give him a quick peck on the lips. His face colours all the way into his receding hairline and she speaks to him quickly, her face only inches from his ear and her brows furrowed. He nods back and tries to pull his hands away, but she doesn't let go.

You swing the door of the taxi closed, worried one of them will see you watching. Calvin is married to a very sensible, if slightly boring, woman called Nadine; you met her at the last Christmas party. You can't imagine that relationship having gone under without leaving a serious mark on Calvin, and coupled with your natural suspicion of Emily, you suspect whatever is happening is going on without Nadine's knowledge.

*

The meeting with Jeremy and the new client goes as smoothly as can be expected. As Candace indicated the whole organisation knows about the poor results Jason was getting. The CEO seemed resistant but Jeremy is certain you can get the relationship back on track.

After you're confident the immediate crisis is over, you rush back to the office to see your next client. There is a message on your voicemail, the client you were supposed to meet at four has cancelled.

You slam the phone down in frustration and instead sliding neatly into place the handset skitters across your desk knocking over a half-empty coffee cup.

"Motherfucker!" you say. It comes out much louder than you expect and you feel your cheeks redden.

"Everything okay out there?" Candace calls from her office, a few metres away.

You mop up the spill as best you can with some tissues and dump the smelly, soggy mess into the bin.

"Sorry, the afternoon isn't really going my way," you reply, your nostrils full of the aroma of stale coffee. You walk over to her office and lean on the door frame.

"I met with Jeremy and that was all fine but very slapdash and so I rushed back here to find my four o'clock had cancelled and then I spilt coffee all over my desk."

You don't mention Emily or Calvin or what you saw getting into the taxi although it's been playing on your mind all afternoon. It seems so out of character for Calvin to be playing around on his wife.

"Thank you for going over there. It's a real help to know I can rely on you." The phone on her desk starts to ring, she looks at the display briefly. "That's Aubrey, I should get this. You go home, Sophie, you've done more than enough work for one day," she says, and you can't help noticing how tired she looks.

Candace is really getting pummelled, you think as you walk over to the kitchen to get a sponge to wipe down your desk properly.

Once it's done a wave of fatigue rolls over you. You reschedule the cancelled meeting and decide to call it a day.

"See you tomorrow," you call out to Candace on your way out. She's still on the phone but she gives you a wave and a thumbs up.

*

On Friday morning you're at your desk working through the background information for this new software client when an email pops up. It's from Emily Sidero. She doesn't usually email you. You're intrigued and open it up immediately.

All yesterday you were on the lookout for anything going on between Emily and Calvin but they were back to behaving as they always did; Calvin in his office alone, door open, and Emily bossing Lola around.

Simon, Here are the figures you wanted. Calvin and I think we've worked out the issues you spotted with line for employee John Smith. Any questions, call my mobile. Emily.

You read and reread the email but you can't make any sense of it. Emily must have typed in the first two letters of the email address and then tabbed into the subject box, but instead of Si for Simon she typed So for Sophie.

You're fairly certain there is no employee called John Smith in the company. With only fifty or so staff you know everyone. To check, you bring up the address book in the email system and search for John. There is not a single John listed.

You open the attached document and realise it's a spreadsheet of every employee in the company, along with various personal details and their salaries. You find your name and the salary listed is correct. You browse through some others, your jaw clenching a little when you see how much Emily makes, much more than you, especially since you don't think she does any work. The next name after Emily is John Smith.

You scroll to his salary and see that it's huge, but he only works one day a week according to this spreadsheet. Even so, his pay is almost $50,000 a year.

He could be some sort of specialist consultant, that would explain the ridiculous rates he's being paid. It could also explain the fact that you've never seen him around, and why isn't on the email list.

CHOOSE:

If you dismiss the email and go back to working, go to p 16.

If you decide to ask Calvin who John Smith is, go to p 32.

C1.1.2 O1 You chose to dismiss the email and go back to working…

You close the email and take a breath. You know that you shouldn't have seen the salary information for the company; wouldn't it be better if you just pretended you hadn't? You could delete the email and if Emily comes to ask you about it, you would tell her that you didn't read it because it wasn't addressed to you.

Just because you don't know who John Smith is doesn't mean he doesn't work here. Aubrey probably has some contacts who do things for him that you're not aware of. You turn your attention back to the spreadsheet you're working on for Jeremy. He's asked you to completely revise the product performance for his whole company.

The vibration of the phone across the desk breaks your concentration. You still coming out tomorrow night? Asks Felicity's text.

The two of you are supposed to be going to a warehouse party down in the Docklands on Saturday night. You've been trying to figure out a way to tell her that it's really not your scene.

I don't really know if I want to. I was going to have a quiet weekend, I've been flat out like a lizard drinking this week, you text back.

Ergh, you're the worst! Alright, you can skip the party but you have to come to dinner and meet Eric. He has a friend, Tom, who will be a third wheel otherwise.

Relief rushes through you. You didn't realise how tense you had been at the idea of going to a warehouse party—the thumping music, sweaty bodies, and pressure to take whatever drugs Felicity is taking. This way you'll get to meet her new boyfriend and be home before midnight.

Okay, sold. Sorry babe.

She sends you details for the restaurant. As you search for the address online, Emily heads to your desk. You concentrate on keeping your face impassive, resisting the urge to scrunch it up.

"Sophie, have you, uh, got a minute?"

"Sure. You wanna sit?" You indicate the chair next to your desk.

"Can we pop into a meeting room?"

You know she wants to talk to you about the email, and probably doesn't want the rest of the office to hear about it, so you agree and follow her into a vacant meeting room.

"I have an awkward admission to make..."

"Okay."

"You may not have seen it, but I sent you an email, it was supposed to go to someone else, and it had highly sensitive payroll information in it. Have you seen it?"

"Uh, was it for someone called Simon?"

"Yes, that's the one. You have seen it then."

"I saw it come through, but I deleted it once I saw it wasn't for me."

"Good. You didn't open the attachment?"

"There was an attachment?" you ask, knowing full well there was and what was in it.

"Yes...I'm glad you haven't seen it. It was pretty sensitive, it could have been a real issue for me if I'd disclosed that to someone outside of the need to know." She seems relieved.

You resent her for making such a huge mistake, even if it seems like an easy slip of the fingers. It's also for the fact that she makes so much more money than you.

"Of course, it would have been really inappropriate for me to open in any case."

"So, uh, you've deleted it?"

"Yes. It's probably still sitting in my deleted folder," you say. "I can delete it out of there too if you like."

"That would be best. I know I can trust you, but better safe than sorry."

"Of course."

You and Emily go back to your desk and she watches as you permanently delete the email. You're fairly sure she doesn't suspect you've seen the salary information, but you will have to be very careful not to let it slip somehow.

Satisfied that she's safe, she wanders back to her desk. Incompetence and arse-covering are added to the list of reasons to dislike Emily along with overly ambitious and mercenary.

The next night, you take the train and walk from Flinders Street station to the restaurant, down near the

Exhibition Buildings. You arrive at the restaurant about fifteen minutes late.

"I'm so sorry, Flick. It was further than I thought. Should have got off at Southern Cross," you say quietly as you hug Felicity hello.

"You're the worst," she says, before stepping back. "This is Eric, and his friend Tom." She waves her hand at the men respectively. Eric is tall, broad-shouldered and you suspect heavily-muscled under his well-fitting suit. He has an unruly mass of blonde curls. Tom is smaller, with dark hair and a piercing gaze. You shake their hands in turn, and stepping closer, you realise that Tom is quite a broad, muscular man in his own right, but next to Eric he seems small. In your mind you start to call him Eric the Viking.

The restaurant is dark, with an unpainted brick interior and exposed light bulbs hanging low over mismatched tables and chairs. Your group sit down and look over the menus. Every meal has a super-food component; quinoa and blueberries and activated almonds and Wagyu beef.

A typically hipster restaurant, you think to yourself.

Tom orders a bottle of expensive white wine to share and you wait for the others to make their selections before you commit to a meal. You want to make sure you fit in with their level of food experimentation.

Felicity orders a salad, Eric orders a steak with a side of bean salad, Tom goes with the burger, and your choice isn't any easier. In the end you go with what you feel like, chicken and ragout with handmade gnocchi.

The conversation flows easily and the wine is delightful but the food is merely passable. Your gnocchi is gummy and the ragout is tasteless, even adding salt doesn't save it.

"How's work then?" Felicity asks. "You said you'd had a bit of a massive week."

"Yeah, I got a new client and there is talk of starting an office in Mackay, which might mean that my boss, Candace, gets transferred up there."

"Would you get her job?" Tom asks, showing interest in the conversation for the first time that night.

"I…" You hesitate. "I guess I'd be on the list. I've only been doing this job for about six months, I transferred from another team. Candace tells me I'm her star performer, but there are others who are much more experienced. She probably says that all her staff are stars. She's very nurturing, if a bit prone to stressing out."

"It doesn't hurt to be ambitious you know, Sophie," Tom says, his dark eyes holding yours for slightly longer than is merely friendly.

"No, I guess not." You look down at your gnocchi, a little unnerved by his forwardness.

In a way Tom is quite attractive, except he seems a bit obsessed with getting ahead at work. He talks at length about how he's going to move up the ranks of the investment firm he works for before branching out into his own consultancy.

"Wouldn't your firm have a problem with you poaching all their clients when you leave?" you ask.

"Well, sure, they have a restraint clause to prevent that, but to be honest, most of those clauses aren't worth the paper they're written on. I'm not worried." He winks at you. You're now feeling quite uncomfortable and your polite smile fades from your face.

I bet he's just as bad in his social settings. Or perhaps he's trying to get the maximum benefit out of people for minimal effort, you think. As you make this realisation, his perfectly proportioned features, striking dark eyes, and luscious head of hair, all lose their allure.

As you finish the meal, the other three prepare to head off to the warehouse party. It's nearly ten o'clock, reasonably late for dinner, and you are very tired. You're quite glad you can to go home to bed, read a book and have an early night.

"So, Sophie." Tom places his hand on the small of your back as you're all standing outside the restaurant waiting for a cab. "I'd be interested in catching up again, one on one, you know. Shall we swap numbers?"

You have no interest in another meeting with Tom in which he lectures you on the best ways to screw people over, but decide it would be confrontational to refuse.

"Sure," you reply, as you and Tom add each other to your phone contact books.

Back at home, you curl up in bed with your trashy horror novel and fall asleep with the book open on your chest.

When you wake, you see Tom and Sophie have both texted you in the wee hours.

Thanks for coming to dinner, I'm going home with Eric. x I'll fill you in later, from Emily at 4:15a.m.

The message from Felicity is her way of telling you she's not likely to join you for brunch. You decide to go on your own. A leisurely morning of your own company will be very nice.

The second message is from Tom, just before one o'clock.

Fantastic to meet you Sophie, you're truly a gorgeous and fascinating woman who I'd like to get to know better. Much better. He signed it with a winky face emoji.

When Tom asked for your number, it was clear he wanted to hook up, and the tone of his text doesn't seem genuine at all. He showed little to no interest in you and he certainly didn't ask you anything that would have led him to conclude you were 'fascinating'. He's buttering you up so you'll sleep with him.

Putting the message from Tom aside, you'll reply to that later, you dress in whatever you have handy.

You head to the café around the corner. The place is packed; Sunday mornings are always busy. Brett, the owner, is English and his broad northern accent makes you giggle. To fit you in, he sits you on a table with another lone customer.

"This is Alfred," he says, affecting an upper class accent. "He's dining alone also." You laugh as Alfred offers his hand to shake.

"Everyone calls me Freddie, except this guy." He smiles at you. It completely alters the impression you had of a brooding and severe man, although his eyes seem a little bit sad.

"I'm sorry to intrude like this," you say, taking a seat opposite him in the corner of the noisy café.

"No trouble," Freddie says, still smiling. "I come here on my own a fair bit and Brett seems to enjoy foisting random patrons on me."

"I haven't had the pleasure before. Usually I come with my friend, Felicity."

"Oh? What's happened to her this week?" His expression is serious again.

"She went to a party last night, I was supposed to go too but decided to be a nanna instead. Anyway she stayed over with her new fella, so I'm here on my own this morning."

"It's nice to be a nanna once in a while. I'm frequently accused of grandpa-ing."

You laugh, somehow the words coming from Freddie's mouth seem incongruous with your impression of him; he's got designer stubble, longish, floppy, brown hair and glasses with thick, square, black frames. As you look closer you notice he's wearing a cardigan.

"The cardi and glasses don't really help your case."

"I can't very well help the state of my eyesight!" he says, in mock outrage. "However, the cardigan is entirely my own doing."

You order eggs and coffee, and Freddie orders the same, with hollandaise sauce and salmon.

Over the excellent brunch, you and Freddie establish an easy rapport, the sort of sincere and yet laidback connection you've struggled to find recently.

Your plates have been cleared away and you are both just about finished your third coffee. It feels like time to start winding things up, but you want to get contact details or set up a follow-up brunch.

Sophie's Path

You toy with your empty coffee glass and brood over how to best arrange this when you realise that Freddie is asking you something.

"What are you doing this afternoon, Sophie Space Cadet?"

"Sorry. I was so busy thinking about how much of a nice time I was having that I forgot to have a nice time." You smile and hope that he'll forgive your awkwardness. "In answer to your question I have nothing on for the afternoon specifically. I mean, I could change my sheets or do the washing up but, that can wait. I'll take almost any offer over any of that."

Freddie smiles, and there is something of the Cheshire cat in the smile. "Well, I suggest we ditch this place before we get caffeine poisoning and go for a stroll around the park?"

You try to figure out what that smile means but it's a lovely day outside, and you decide to go with it. "Sure, that sounds cool. Delightful even."

You both settle your bills before heading out into the mild autumn sunshine. The air is relatively still and the weak sunlight warms you. By the time you get to the park you're even sweating a little.

"It's a gorgeous day, but it's a bit hot for a cardi," Freddie says, taking off the cardigan and tying it around his waist. The gesture makes him look as though he's back at school and you giggle quietly.

"You're right, but I'm not wearing anything that can be taken off!" You pick up the front of your top and flap it away from your body, trying to create some air flow.

Freddie looks away as you flap. It's certainly a good sign that he wants to spend more time with you, even though you just met.

"Shall we find a bench on the shade?" you suggest as Freddie turns back to face you.

"Let's!"

The park is narrow but long, it runs down between groups of houses, probably land set aside for some obsolete purpose, such as a railway line. There is a children's playground and a bike path that runs the length of the park, creating a sense of constant action. You and Freddie are the only people who don't seem to be going somewhere.

"What about this grassy knoll?" Freddie says finally, pointing to a raised section of turf near a large plane tree.

"That should do nicely." You sit down on the grass and wriggle your bottom into a comfortable sitting position before Freddie lays down his cardigan and takes a seat next to you. You notice that he has chosen to sit closer than is strictly necessary.

Your mind keeps straying to the bare skin of his arm that is almost, but not quite, touching yours. You can feel the warmth coming from him, or perhaps it's your imagination.

Freddie has large tattoos down his arms, which were not visible under the cardigan, but you can see them coming down out of the sleeves of his T-shirt.

"Nice ink," you say, struggling for something to say now you're preoccupied with his naked forearm. You resist the urge to reach out to touch them.

"Oh, thanks," he says. "They're from my somewhat misspent youth. Now that I'm a grownup I tend not to show them off, except when it's hot."

"Do you regret getting them?" you ask.

"No, not at all. I'd never have them removed, they're a reminder of the person I used to be, not who I want to be now. If that makes sense."

You look at him without saying anything else, hoping he'll want to fill the silence with the rest of the story.

"Alright...I used to be in a heavy metal band. We were moderately successful. We were all law students and after I finished my undergrad, I toured with the band solidly for about a year before the cracks started to show. The singer really got into coke and we had trouble getting him to turn up to gigs." He drops his head back onto the grass.

"And I was starting to get tired of the nomadic lifestyle, I missed my family and friends back here in Melbourne. The drinking and groupies were just not cutting it as a substitute, so it sort of disintegrated."

You catch him looking at you from the corner of his eye.

"Mmm," you say.

"The guitarist and bass player got together after the band broke up and they live on a hobby farm in the Yarra Valley. I dunno what happened to Marco, the singer. Maybe I should try to track him down..."

As he's talking, you turn it over in your mind, but no matter which way you look at it you can't figure Freddie for a drummer in a metal band.

"Sounds like an exciting phase of your life, but it doesn't tell me why you got the tatts or why you don't feel like they're you now."

Freddie smiles and gives a small sigh. "You're right. I got them while I was still studying, spent the money we made at gigs on them over about a year. I thought it made me seem tough. I..." he stares away over your shoulder before going on. "I didn't feel like I belonged in that world, I was a closet grandpa and they were my way of telling myself it was legit."

"But now you've accepted your inner grandpa?"

He laughs. "You could say that. I still jam sometimes with people but, I'm not really cut out to be a rock star. I'm cut out to be a fabulous office manager, a good cook and a passable gardener."

"That sounds nice," you say absently. You lie back on the grass and close your eyes for a long moment, thinking about Freddie's story.

When you open your eyes Freddie's face is right next to yours, he's leaning back on his elbow and looking at you with an intense expression. You flinch, startled by his closeness.

You know you should say something. You could share something of your past, but you don't want to make it about you.

Instead you decide to close your eyes again and hope that Freddie takes the opportunity to kiss you. You breathe deeply into your belly, and project your desire into the universe. You start to count your breaths and wait.

Sophie's Path

When you get to twenty-five you sneak a look out of the corner of your eye and see that Freddie has lain back down on the grass next to you.

I guess I'll have to do it myself, my psychic message was not clear enough, you think as you lean over Freddie's peaceful upturned face. As you get nearer to him you smell the grass and the remnants of coffee in his breath. There is another subtle scent too, probably body wash or shampoo rather than cologne.

As you hover over him, your lips an inch from his, he flicks open his eyes. He grins that surprising grin and lifts his mouth up to meet yours.

It starts slowly, each of you pressing your lips against the others' almost innocently. Then you start to explore, dipping your tongue into his mouth.

Your urgency builds, at first it's you above him, leaning on his chest, and then he's rolled you over and is pressing himself onto you, his thighs pressed heavily between your legs.

You just want to stay in this embrace. Freddie winds his arm around your waist to bring you closer to him, you can feel his erection pushing itself between you, but you leave your hands on his back and he does the same.

You feel intoxicated. Eventually the need to laugh makes its way to the surface and you have to turn your face away, so as not to laugh while kissing him.

"What's funny?" he asks.

"I don't know!" you say, helpless to stop the shaking that starts in your belly and seems to travel right through you.

"I've never had this reaction. I might be inclined to feel offended."

"Oh, no, don't! It's just, I don't know, I feel strangely happy and it's making me giggle. It's not a reflection on your technique"—you pause—"well, not in a bad way."

Freddie leans over and kisses you again. His hand slides down your back to grab your arse, and you think perhaps you should move somewhere less public.

"I live just around the corner, if that's something you, err, were interested in seeing," he says, that Cheshire cat grin back on his face. You don't even have to think about it.

It's true that Freddie's place is just around the corner, in less than five minutes you're approaching the apartment block where he lives. It's a new looking building and it still has that sterile feeling about it of excessively neat gardens and pristine grey walls. His apartment is two bedrooms, and he lives with a woman called Jessie, he tells you, who is away for the weekend with her girlfriend. "It's not as expensive as it seems, I promise."

"How did you guess?"

"Everyone wants to know how I afford the rent, and that's the short answer, I don't!" He steps towards you wrapping you in his arms and walking you backwards to the couch.

His couch is cream faux suede, boxy and hard. It's a little too short to make out on. You can't seem to find the right position and keep shuffling awkwardly, while trying not to break the kiss.

Sophie's Path

You turn away and spot the open door leading to the bedroom. You take Freddie's hand and lead him there, hoping it's the right one. You stand at the foot of the bed and kiss him hard on the mouth, running your hands up inside his T-shirt, then slip it up over his head.

His urgency returns and his greedy hands run all over your body, fumbling, trying to get to your skin. You peel off the layers of your clothing slowly.

Once you're both naked you explore each other carefully, wanting to draw out the moment. The sex itself seems like less of a goal now than spending time pleasuring each other. You run your fingers over his chest, getting to know the slight covering of hair and the lean muscles there.

When you finally get to penetration it's almost more than you can stand. You've never been so turned on.

"You feel so good." You sigh.

Afterwards as you lie next to him, panting a little as your breathing returns to its normal pace, you turn to him. He's staring at the ceiling.

"Thank you," he whispers, not looking away from the spot above him.

"What for?"

"For sitting with me at brunch." He sits up on one elbow and turns his intense stare towards you. "Otherwise I wouldn't never have been able to do this." He kisses you gently but insistently, inflaming your desire for him once more.

Fleur Blüm

You found the right man and you grabbed the
opportunity! You win!

The End.

C1.1.2 O2 You chose to ask Calvin who John Smith is…

You decide that it's not worth scheming and wondering about it too much, there must be a reasonable explanation of who John Smith is. You consider your options, you should tell Emily that you got an email not addressed to you; you don't have to tell her you read the attachment. You want to know who John Smith is, but you can't ask her about it. You decide it's best to forget about it.

You send off a quick reply to Emily alerting her to the mistake and get back to reading over the new client information. But you can't concentrate, you want to know who John Smith is so badly it's all you can think about.

You stand up at your desk and check that Emily is not around. The only person you feel you can ask is Calvin.

Calvin has worked in the Payroll department of the company for years, you're not sure how long, but well before you started five years ago. He's a bit of an enigma, very quiet and serious in his work, doesn't attend many company functions but always brings his wife, Nadine, to the Christmas party. She's a very severe-looking woman, and you create an imaginary world for them in which they watch nature documentaries and drink one glass of red wine after dinner because it's good for the heart.

You get up and walk over to Calvin's office.

"Hey Calvin, have you got a minute?" As soon as you start speaking you realise you don't really have a plan.

"Yeah, sure, pull up a seat." Calvin has always been friendly when you drop by for a chat although he'd never start a conversation with you of his own accord.

"I…" You take a deep breath, "I came across some documentation referring to an employee, John Smith, I guess he must be a consultant or something coz I've never heard of him, and I…wanted to, well, I wanted to know who he is."

You look at Calvin directly. You try to breathe evenly and smooth your face into an approximation of friendly interest. You're sure that Calvin can hear your heart beating; it's certainly loud in your own ears. Calvin looks away to his computer screen.

"Oh, John? You haven't heard about him?" Calvin's voice seems more high-pitched than usual.

"Nope, I never have until today," you say, letting Calvin pull himself together in his own time.

"I just do what I'm told, I've only met him once, but I think he's doing something with Aubrey. He told me all about the project; something to do with where the company is heading and how to manage the new growth. You must have noticed that our client base is getting much bigger these days and we'll have to start thinking about what changes need to be made to accommodate and best serve all the clients."

Two things stick out about Calvin's reply, firstly it's long-winded, and secondly it's meaningless. Either he doesn't know what John Smith does and is trying to cover himself, or there's something about the arrangement that makes him uncomfortable.

"Does he ever come into the office?" You decide to push this line a little further.

"No, only once to give me his forms," Calvin admits.

"Is that unusual?"

"You'd have to ask Aubrey. I don't like to ask that sort of thing myself." Calvin picks up a pile of papers from his desk and straightens them. "Anyway, uh, I'm a bit busy. Pay day is next Tuesday and I have a bit of work that I need to be getting on with…" He trails off. You're sure he wants you to leave, but there is something he's not saying.

"Of course, sorry. I…thanks for having a chat with me."

You go back to your desk and Calvin closes his office door. He doesn't usually close it, and perhaps he is just getting on with the payroll, but together with what you saw on Wednesday you decide to keep your eye on things between Emily and Calvin, and especially regarding John Smith.

*

Over the weekend you go to a warehouse party with Felicity and spend most of the night watching her make out with Eric, a tall blond man. On Sunday you spend the day with your parents, and it's as typically uneventful as it usually is. Monday and Tuesday are spent at the offices of the new software client, trying to make sense of what they want out of the relationship now you've taken over from Jason.

When you arrive early on Wednesday morning Candace calls you into her office.

I bet she needs me to present her material to the meeting again, you think as you walk over to her.

"Close the door will you, please?" Candace says. Her tone is formal and her mouth is compressed into a tight line.

"Sure." You take a seat facing her desk; the chair is less comfortable than it appears.

"There's…there's no easy way to tell you this. The thing is, there's been a complaint made about you." Candace doesn't meet your eye.

"What do you mean, a complaint?" You sit up straighter in your uncomfortable chair, you can feel the adrenalin starting to flow into your body.

"It's an allegation of sexual harassment. We're taking it quite seriously, although obviously you're innocent until proven otherwise. Calvin Pryce is alleging that you've been leaving pornographic material on his desk, sending inappropriate emails and making lewd suggestions."

You laugh; it must be some sort of joke, but Candace's expression remains serious.

"Me? Harass Calvin?" you say.

"Yes. HR is already in the process of investigating it."

You look down at your hands and pick a piece of fluff from your skirt while you try to get your mind around what's happening.

"Right," you say finally. "What happens now?"

"The thing is, they, I mean HR, have asked that you go home, on full pay, of course, while they conduct their investigation. You'll have your chance to reply to the complaint, of course, you'll be able to put forward your case." Candace is wringing her hands unconsciously as she talks.

"Go home? Starting from when? What about my clients? What about the new client I've just spend two days soothing?"

"You'll need to leave straight away I'm afraid. You're to leave your laptop and any other company property you have with you here in the office. They'll have to go through your things. I'll be taking over the new client, and distributing your other work across the team until you're back."

"This is a nightmare," you say.

"I know, I'm really sorry. We have to take this sort of thing seriously. I don't believe that you would do what they're accusing you of, but they can't just take my word for it."

You fight down an urge to laugh. Surely this is some horrible joke, and you'll walk out of the building and everyone will yell surprise.

"I'll be off then." You're suddenly very angry, your fingernails are digging into your palms; if it is a joke it's in very poor taste. You want to be out of the building as soon as possible.

"Please try to stay positive. We'll get to the bottom of this in a jiffy and you'll be back here before you know it."

"Yeah. Sure." You stand up and stalk out of the room, your hands clenched at your sides.

You pick up your bag, loudly slamming the file you had in it onto the desk and leave the office without saying a word to anyone. You wonder how many people know about the accusations; there's hardly a person in the office who looks at you.

Once you're out of the building and walking down the street towards the tram stop you start to feel cold and sick. Was it the conversation you had about John Smith, the probably fictional consultant, that caused Calvin to fabricate accusations of harassment? You wouldn't have thought he had it in him, but maybe you don't really know what he's like; sneaking around with Emily and hiding employees.

You want to call Felicity but she's at work and probably won't be able to talk.

Call me as soon as you have a minute. Shit has hit the fan. You text her.

You arrive home about an hour later and there has been no response from Flick. You don't know what to do with your time you can't even get on with work at home, so you do the first thing that comes to mind; go back to bed.

You are startled awake by the sound of your phone ringing. You don't remember falling asleep; it felt like you lay in your bed for hours waiting for sleep or for a better idea to come, and now you feel groggy. You fumble for your phone, which is still in your handbag, and just answer before the call goes to voicemail.

"Hello?"

"Sophie? Are you okay?" Felicity's concern breaks through your fogginess.

"It's all fucked."

"What's happened?"

You start to tell her everything and immediately burst into tears. You continue, hiccoughing and sniffling as you struggle to talk through your tears.

"I don't know what to say. That's terrible… it's all just really awful," she says when you finish.

"I know."

"I have to get back to work, but, uh, I'll come by tonight?"

You look at your watch, it's only just after two in the afternoon. "No, I just want to be alone right now."

"Uh, alright. If you change your mind you know where I am. Call me as soon as you hear anything, alright?"

"Okay."

"Promise me."

"Yes, I promise."

"Love you." The call drops out.

You decide to treat yourself to an afternoon of catching up on all the T.V. you haven't been able to watch recently. You binge watch three films on the SBS website on your laptop in bed. As it starts to get dark and your belly complains about the lack of lunch, you walk ten minutes down the road to the supermarket.

You tell yourself that you're allowed one day to wallow in self-pity and stock up on junk food: corn chips, lollies, chocolate and two bottles of cheap white wine. As you walk home with your laden shopping bags, you text Felicity.

No news. Am drowning my sorrow in junk food and wine.

Sorry to hear no progress. Want to talk about it? she texts back.

No, I'm okay. I'll call you tomorrow.

In the morning, you're woken by the ringing of your phone. You forgot to turn off your alarm, but immediately turned it off and went back to sleep. You search through the tangle bed clothes to find it.

"Hello," you say.

"Yes, hello. Is that Sophie Faithful?"

"Speaking," you say. The man on the phone is speaking very loudly given the amount of wine you drank last night. You squint your eyes as though that helps.

"This is Joseph Sargeant, from the Human Resources Department, I'm sure we've met. I'm calling to set up a time to have a chat with you about a complaint which has been made against you."

You've only met Joseph once or twice at social functions. He processed your transfer into Candace's team but it was mostly via email.

"What exactly is the content of the complaint? Can I have a look at it before the meeting?" Your adrenaline has kicked in and you can feel your hands trembling.

"Uh, yes, well, that's part of the reason for calling the meeting. It's not something we like to discuss over the phone. I'm sorry you've had to be removed from the office, but we've always found it easier to handle things this way."

Easier for him, perhaps, you think. You clench your teeth and wait for him to go on.

"So, uh, anyway," Joseph says. "Can you come in this afternoon?"

"I would normally be working, so I have no other plans." You glance at the clock and see it's just after ten o'clock. The tremors in your hands are starting to subside leaving the cold, seething anger in the pit of your stomach.

"Yes. Of course."

You hear him clicking his mouse in the background and the murmurs of the office.

"What about two?"

"That's fine."

"We'll have to meet outside the office, so I've arranged for us to use the chambers of the law firm we –"

"I beg your pardon?" You cut him off. "When did lawyers get involved? It feels like you're deliberately leaving me in the dark here. I don't feel like my feelings are really being taken into consideration. Should I speak to the union?"

You wonder who exactly the union rep is, but you decide not to ask Joseph.

"I understand it's a very difficult position to be in. In terms of support, you're entitled to have someone present in the meeting to act as a support person. You can choose to have a friend, partner, or a representative from the union. It's still all quite preliminary, but we do try to do things by the book."

You bark out a harsh laugh. "By the book. Right. What's the address then?"

Joseph gives you the address and you hang up quickly.

CHOOSE:

If you choose to take a representative from the union go to <u>p 42.</u>

If you choose to take Felicity, go to <u>p 64.</u>

C1.1.3 O1 You chose to take a representative from the union…

You decide your best bet is to ask someone from the union. You search online for the contact details and finally find an organiser who seems to deal with your company. His name is Bruce Toro and when he answers the phone he sounds angry. No, more like belligerent.

"Bruce here," he says.

"Hi Bruce. My name is Sophie and I…have a situation that I think I might need your help with."

"I see. And you're a member are you?"

"Yes."

"Okay. So tell me about this situation." The way he says situation makes you very uncomfortable.

You try not to burst into tears as you explain; you don't think Bruce would be particularly comforting if you started crying.

"I've been asked to a meeting today and I really don't know what to do," you say.

"You've come to the right place. I can come this afternoon, but I don't have much time to spend with you beforehand. We'll have to wing it but I'm sure it will become clear that the claims are vexatious."

"Right. I'll see you there?"

"Yep, see you there."

You hang up and immediately feel as though you've made a mistake. Bruce isn't comforting, and he didn't seem particularly interested in hearing what you had to say. You hope he doesn't try to run the meeting off the rails by making it about some agenda he's pushing.

The building where the industrial relations lawyers' offices are is in Spring Street at the top of the CBD. Apart from you, there is Joseph, and a woman called Germaine Spitznogle.

Two minutes before the meeting is about to begin a man storms through the foyer towards you. He's well over six feet tall and has wide shoulders and very little neck. His black hair is in a crew cut and the hairline is very close to his eyebrows, making his forehead short and giving him a Neanderthal appearance.

"Bruce Toro. You must be Sophie." He sticks out an enormous hand to shake yours. His grip is far too tight and you wince.

"Let's get started then." He doesn't wait for confirmation of who you are, and strides through the open door of the boardroom.

Bruce thumps a stack of papers down on the table.

"Bruce." Joseph stands to shake his hand, they've clearly met before.

"Joe."

Joseph grimaces at the nickname, his fingers tightening slightly around the folder he's holding. "Take a seat, please. This is my colleague Germaine Spitznogle."

"Now that we're all here, I remind you that you're a spectator only. All questions will be directed to and should be answered by Sophie," Germaine says, looking at Bruce.

Bruce scoffs. "I know how these things work, thank you. I've been a union organiser for ten years. I've kept up with the legislation that allows employers to bully and harass their employees, to get more out of them than they are paying for, to watch the hard-won gains of the eighties and nineties go down the toilet with various employment law reforms. I expect I know at least as much about it as you do, Ms Spitznogle."

You're not impressed with the implied sexism in Bruce's statement, and you wonder if you've made a mistake asking him to come.

Joseph starts going through the complaint. Your heart sinks as Calvin's claims pile up, one on top of the next. He has copies of emails allegedly sent from you to Calvin with explicit and entirely inappropriate content.

"I need to put a brake on this meeting for a moment," Bruce says. "This evidence needs to be carefully looked over, and, now that we've heard the claims in full, I'd like a chance to talk to Sophie about them and the possibilities going forward. What are the disciplinary outcomes on the table?"

Joseph blinks rapidly before he answers. "Well, if the claims are found to be true, given their nature, the company would be looking to terminate Sophie's employment. Effective immediately, with four weeks of gardening leave."

"And if the claims are found to be unsubstantiated, or worse vexatious, as is Sophie's assertion, what is the company's position then?"

"We would obviously have to look very seriously at Calvin and determine an appropriate disciplinary course for making a false claim."

"Alright. Could Sophie and I have a few minutes?"

Germaine looks at Joseph and inclines her head slightly to the door.

"Yes, that's fine, we can give you the room," he says.

Bruce waits until the door is firmly closed before starting. "You said that the claims are spurious, but these emails seem to show otherwise. What's the story here? You were sleeping with him and he's suddenly decided he's sick of it?"

You're so angry you can't seem to form words, only make spluttering noises.

"If you did it, you have to 'fess up. I can't help you if you continue to deny it. We can probably get them to pay you out eight weeks if you agree to resign. It looks like a solid case they've got." Bruce prods the email printouts; you glance at them and they're as explicit as they are poorly written. You would never write anything like that nor could you say that you did.

"I did not do this. Those emails are fake. I will not admit to something I didn't do," you say, your voice cold.

"That's all well and good that you want to stick to that story, but unless you can prove these emails were doctored, which I doubt you can, I'd just cop to it and take the package." Bruce leans back in his chair, not interested in what you're telling him.

"I want to keep my job. I don't want to have this on my employment record. This is a nightmare," you say, knowing you're talking to yourself.

Germaine and Joseph knock on the door and come back in.

"I'm sorry we couldn't give you longer but Germaine has another appointment after this one and we want to be able to wrap this up as quickly as we can." Joseph walks around the table to take his seat. His jaw is rippling as he clenches and unclenches it. If he had hackles, you expect they would be raised. You don't like how this is going.

"So, we've discussed some things," Bruce begins. "Sophie is willing to resign effective immediately, with eight weeks' gardening leave, and a statement of service. Is that something can agree to?"

You're speechless. This isn't what you thought you'd agreed to.

Joseph stops clenching his jaw and looks at Germaine, who nods. "I think that solution would be agreeable to everyone," he says.

"But I didn't do this," you say.

"That doesn't matter. This is the best you're going to get," Bruce hisses. "Just take it and move on to something better."

"We'll draw up an agreement for you to sign, Sophie, and we'll mail it to you. You'll just need to sign it and send it back. With regards to collecting your things, we can probably arrange for that to happen in a couple of weeks when things are settled down. I'll tell the staff that you're on personal leave and will not be returning," Joseph says.

You walk out of the meeting defeated and slightly nauseated. Bruce just resigned on your behalf and you didn't say anything to stop him.

As you head home on the tram, your depression turns to anger. You can't bear to call Felicity and tell her what happened. It feels like your fault things went so badly.

When you get home, you lie on your couch and start to cry, softly at first but with increasing intensity until your whole body is shaking and your eyes are swollen and painful.

Eventually you wipe your face on your sleeve as exhaustion takes primary position in your body and your tears dry up.

When you finally call Felicity it goes through to her voicemail. It's only four o' clock, she's at work. You're sitting at home, the curtains drawn and the lights off, with snot on your sleeve.

"I don't have a job. Everything's fallen apart. Call me back."

You drop the phone next to the couch and close your eyes.

The sound of your phone ringing startles you awake again. You open your eyes, which feel gritty and blurry.

"Flick?" you say.

"What the fuck happened?"

"He'd faked emails between us and the union guy told them I'd resign if they paid me out eight weeks. I just sat there and let him do it. I don't have a job, I'm not allowed back in the office. Aubrey will hate me, Candace will hate me. What am I going to say to Max?"

"Oh babe, I'm so sorry. This is so fucked. I'm coming over right now, okay?"

"No one will give me a reference after this. How will I get another job?" You're not listening to Felicity.

"Sophie? I'm coming now, I'll be half an hour. Will you be at home?" she asks, as though you were a child.

"Yes, I'm on the couch. Bring wine. Lots of wine."

"Okay. I'll see you soon."

She hangs up and you drop the phone back on the floor. You try to get back to sleep but it seems like the moment has gone. Tears leak from your eyes again and roll down into your ears as you stare up at the ceiling.

How did it get to this? You want to say it's all Bruce's fault, but if Calvin hadn't made those claims, if you'd left John Smith alone, if Emily hadn't sent you that email, if they hadn't been so close in the meeting. The start of the shit storm was seeing them at that meeting.

Felicity buzzes your intercom half an hour later. "Let me in!" she says through the tinny speaker.

You press the button to let her up and unlatch your front door before slinking back to the couch.

Felicity comes straight in, putting down the wine she brought with her, and comes to hug you. You don't have the energy to hug her back, you sit awkward and limp as she embraces you.

"I'm going to pour you a glass of wine," Felicity says.

"Thank you," is all you can manage to reply.

*

48

After that night you indulge yourself in misery for a few days. Felicity checks in with you each evening and you find that your anger has started to dissipate, but your disappointment remains. You consider emailing Candace and Max, but you decide that would be too impersonal.

Calling Max seems like the best thing to start with. You have his mobile number stored in your phone and you figure it's probably better not to call the office line.

"Yes, Max here," he says as he answers your call.

"It's Sophie," you say, pausing so that Max can get his head around it.

"Sophie! My God! We…" he trails off.

"I know. I'm so sorry. I wanted to tell you, but it all happened so fast."

"That makes sense. I want to have a proper talk, but I think I should step out of the office. Can I call you back in two minutes?"

It's the longest two minutes of your life before Max finally calls you back.

"So what the fuck happened?" he says as you pick up.

"I'm not supposed to tell anyone. I signed a confidentiality agreement."

"Screw the agreement, I thought we were friends. I don't need to know details, just broad strokes, but one minute you're here on the fast track up and the next minute you're gone."

"That wasn't my choice," you begin. "There were some allegations of… a complaint was made, about me—"

"By who? I'll kill 'em."

"I can't tell you that. It all came about because of an email I received by mistake about some…financial irregularities, and when I asked questions I was thrown under the bus."

"Jesus," he says in a sigh.

"In the end, it was decided that it would be best for me to resign effective immediately and no one would say any more about it."

"Right. I wouldn't have thought Calvin had it in him. I'm sure it wasn't his idea."

"I didn't say any of that…I wouldn't have thought he was up to it either, but here we are."

You're both silent for a while, you can hear the trams rumbling by on Collins Street; Max must me having a smoke while he's on the phone. He said he'd quit smoking, but this probably counts as serious enough to deserve a small lapse.

"So, what now?" he asks, you hear him breathing out in a long sigh, confirming your suspicions of a cigarette.

"I don't really know. Some time feeling sorry for myself I think. Most of all I feel sad I couldn't tell everyone goodbye. Not even you or Candace." Your voice starts to tremble and you bite your tongue to stop yourself from crying again.

"Of course you do. I can't believe they forced you to resign in disgrace because of political bullshit."

"Yeah…I'm trying to look forwards, not backwards. But, I have an awkward question to ask. Would you act as my referee?"

"In an instant."

"But please, please, if they ask why I left, just say I resigned and you don't know anything else about it. Can you promise me?"

You hear Max hurrumphing down the phone. "Yes, alright, I'll be suitably vague about the whole thing."

"Thank you." You sigh.

"Are you applying for things yet?"

"Not yet. I've hardly had the time to look," you say, you don't add that you've been too busy drowning your sorrows and sleeping.

"Just let me know when you need me to talk you up." A tram dings loudly in the background. "I should probably get back to work, I'll talk to you soon," Max says.

Putting the phone down, you look down at yourself and realise that you're sitting in pyjamas that you've been wearing for two days straight. You shower and put on clean clothes before calling Candace. It goes through to voicemail.

"Hi Candace. It's Sophie. Uh...can you call me back?"

Knowing the pressure she was under before you were forced to resign, no doubt she's completely snowed under, now having to recruit a replacement for you, soothing your clients, and managing your workload. It will probably take her some time to get back to you, and no doubt she'll want to do it when there aren't many people around to overhear her.

*

Sophie's Path

The café around the corner from your house does very nice coffee and eggs, you decide to try that for lunch while you wait for Candace's call. Brett, the manager, greets you warmly when you walk in. He's balding, red-headed and lanky, and his accent is pure Liverpool. You love to listen to him.

"We don't usually see you of a weekday," he says as he hands you a menu. You sit in the shaded courtyard out the back.

"I'm what you might call between jobs just at the minute." The hollow feeling in your chest is back, you push it down.

"You'll be right love, something'll turn up."

You take a seat and enjoy the sunshine on your face. It's cool, but the courtyard is enclosed so there's no wind, the late autumn sun is pleasantly warm. You order chicken pasta and a coffee.

There are one or two other people sitting in the café courtyard. One of them is an older gent reading the paper, a flat cap on his head you suspect is hiding his lack of hair, and another is a guy about your age who seems to be working. He has a laptop in front of him, and a notepad and papers beside him. Occasionally he takes a sip from his latte, or a bite from his focaccia, though he seems so absorbed in his work you doubt he tastes either of them.

"Here we are. Nourishment for the idle soul." Brett places the meal in front of you.

"That's my mate, Alfred, in case you're interested." Brett looks over to the guy with the laptop. Alfred absently sweeps his hair back. "He works too hard in my opinion. You should go and distract him."

How did he know? Was I staring? you ask yourself. You look over again and Alfred seems to have a very intense attraction about him. His dark, straight hair would hang into his eyes if it weren't for the thick black-rimmed glasses that seem to catch it. The expression on his face, furrowed brow with a pen in his mouth, is pure concentration.

You look away and try to occupy yourself with your pasta, but after several days shut up in your apartment you find your eyes drawn back again and again to Alfred.

When Brett comes back to collect your plate, you put your hand on his arm. "Does he come in often?"

"Oh yeah. Almost every day. Don't remember what he does for a crust, but he seems to like doing it at our tables." He winks at you again. You wish he wouldn't, it makes you feel as though you're doing something naughty.

"Hi," you say on a whim as you head towards the door.

He looks up from his computer and you think he's about to say something cutting before his expression softens.

"I was just having lunch and I saw that you were eating alone, so I was wondering, if you are going to be here tomorrow?" You feel like an idiot. "And if you are, would you like some company?" Your heart is pounding so loudly in your ears you're sure he can hear it too.

He frowns for a long time, the line between his eyebrows is deep; he's probably an angry guy and is going to tell you to mind your own business.

"Actually, that sounds lovely." Then he smiles at you and it changes everything about him. The brooding impression of anger is swept away as his eyes crinkle in delight.

"I usually get here about twelve and it takes me about two hours to have lunch and get some work done. It's the most productive time in my day because nobody can interrupt me, I refuse to tell the office where I go," he adds.

"Oh. You don't have to eat with me, you know if you need to get stuff done, I totally understand. I just thought you...might want some company."

He laughs. "It's fine. Brett tells me I work too hard. I probably do." His eyes flick back to his screen.

"I'll see you tomorrow then," you say, backing away. You almost bump into Brett who winks, again. You roll your eyes and head out the front and home.

Inspired by the successful lunch invitation you get into job hunting when you get home. You trawl through ads for a good few hours before realising it's getting dark. By the end of the night you've sent off a few applications for jobs that you're not really qualified for, but which sound like an interesting next step in your career.

Felicity calls to check in that evening. "Hi!"

"You sound very perky. Did you have a good day?" she asks.

"I did, actually. Called Max, then took myself out for lunch and I have a lunch date for tomorrow. Well, I'm hoping it's a date. I even applied for a couple of jobs."

"Sounds fab, babe. I just went to boring work and did boring work things. Day after tomorrow you should come in and have lunch with me!" she says.

"Yes, deal...the only thing I didn't get done was speaking to Candace; she's probably totally overwhelmed at work without me." It sounds conceited when you say it out loud but you know it's true.

"You'll get onto her in the end. She seemed to be pretty pleased with your work in general before...well, you know."

"Yeah," you say, your voice flat.

"Sorry, babe, I didn't mean to bring you down."

"It's okay. I'm just tired, I haven't been sleeping so well." You stifle a yawn and rub your eyes. "I'm gonna have an early night."

"Alright, I'll call you tomorrow. I want general details about the possibly lunch date and you can fill me in on the finer points at lunch on Friday."

As much as you want it to be a date, you don't know if he does. And if it was a date you would have to stress out about it. You tell yourself, again, that it isn't a date.

*

In the morning you wash and style your hair, and put on some subtle but confidence boosting makeup. You decide to wear one of the dresses you usually save for semi-formal dinners and job interviews; it's various shades of purple and falls in swishy diaphanous waves around you, and a nice black cardigan, in case the weather isn't as pleasant today as it was yesterday.

You walk into the café at just after 12:30p.m., and Alfred is sitting at the same table in the courtyard. He doesn't have his laptop with him and he looks vulnerable and naked without it. He smiles as he sees you, lifting that intense expression again. You wonder if that's the way his face falls, and feel like you've judged him too early.

He stands up as you join him, sticking his hand out to shake yours.. "Hello, that's very formal," you say as you take his hand.

"Yes, it's a bit of a reflex."

You settle into a hard-backed café chair across the table from where he sits on a padded bench. "So, Alfred, no laptop today?"

"Yes, I left it in the office. I decided to switch off completely." He looks at his phone on the table, and picks it up, sliding it into his pants pocket. "I did bring the phone, so I'll try very hard not to check emails on there. Oh, and call me Freddie, no one calls me Alfred. Except Brett, who thinks it's funny."

"He seems to live in a world where he's hilarious. I'm not sure it has much in common with reality though."

Freddie laughs and you lean back, playing with your hair.

"So," he says.

"So! Here we are."

"Yes. What brings you here on a weekday? I don't think I've seen you before."

"No. I've recently finished a job in the city so I'm not working just at the moment, which means I'm free to come to my local for lunch with myself. Or with charming gentlemen."

His cheeks turn a slightly pinker shade. "Ah, I've been in places like that, especially when a contract ends and I haven't had another one to go onto."

You don't say anything, and after a couple of beats, Freddie picks up his thread again.

"I work for the local Greens' member, her office is just around the corner and I live a few blocks the other way." He sweeps his arm in the direction of the park. "So I may as well live here."

"What do you do for the Greens? Sounds exciting."

"It sounds exciting, but it's not really." He tells you about his job, and just as he is heading into a level of detail that is moderately boring, Brett comes over to take your orders.

"You chatterboxes want anything to eat yet?" he says.

"Oh, goodness, I haven't even looked," you say, quickly grabbing the menu.

"I'll have the usual," Freddie says.

"Latte and chicken focaccia," says Brett.

"I'll have the same," you say instantly, passing the menu back to Brett.

You wonder if Freddie thinks it's weird that you want to have the same as him, but as soon as he'd said it you knew it was what you felt like.

Now that you're sitting with him, you allow yourself to really stare at his face. It's noble, with strong brows, nose and jaw line. Self-assured without being arrogant. The sort of confidence that you associate with people who are secure being around talented people. He's not wearing his glasses today, and he looks quite different without them.

You eat and chat about this and that, and the time seems to fly by.

He pulls his phone out of his pocket. "Sorry, I'm just checking the time, I have a meeting at three."

"You did well not to go for it before now," you say. You glance at your watch and it's after two.

As he registers the time and whatever else has happened on his phone in the interim, he says, "wow, it got to two o'clock quickly. I'd better dash."

"Of course, of course. You have to get back to work. I, as a lady of leisure, do not."

"I'm very jealous."

"Don't be," you say in a low voice.

Freddie collects his satchel and stands up. He hovers for a moment, as you stand up and then goes in to give you a hug. It's warm and gentle, and allows you to feel the lean musculature of his body. You smell him as you hug him back, sort of citrusy, subtle like a body wash or shampoo rather than a cologne. He steps back, breaking the embrace.

"Here's my card," he says, fumbling the rectangle of cardboard from his back pocket. "That's my personal phone number as well as the work line. We'll have to set up something to hang out again."

"Thanks very much, I'll text you." You take the card, he's written his mobile number on it by hand.

"Okay. See you," he says waving briefly before disappearing back through the café.

You sit down again and order a chai latte. You enjoy the afterglow of the hug for as long as you can, but eventually you get restless to head home. You're not sure what you'll do with rest of the afternoon, maybe a spring clean is in order.

"Alfred covered the tab, except for that last chai," Brett says when you go to pay.

"That's very sweet of him."

As you walk home you text Freddie's number. "You shouldn't have paid for lunch. How about I get the next one? Dinner on Saturday?"

You feel a wave of anxiety as soon as the text is sent; knowing that if someone asked you to dinner on a Saturday, that would definitely be a date. In all that talking you never even asked if he was single.

Oh well, it's done now, you tell yourself.

When you get home you flop down on your sofa and switch on the T.V.. There's nothing on, but you want to relish the moment, to relive looking into his vast blue eyes.

You're still watching T.V. when Felicity calls you later that night. It's getting dark outside without you noticing and you're lit only by the glow of the screen.

"So?" she says as soon as you answer.

"What?" you reply.

"Tell me!"

"You said you wanted to wait till tomorrow…"

"I know what I said. I can't take it. Tell me now."

"Alright then." You go over the lunch meeting in exquisite detail.

"Any reply to the text?" she asks when you're done.

"Umm." You pull the phone away from your ear to check it in case something came through while you were talking. "Not so far."

You hear the disappointment in your own voice, but you know that he is a workaholic and might be still on the job. It's only 7p.m.

"He'll send you something eventually. Anyway, I'm gonna go, I'm starving. Don't forget lunch with me tomorrow. You have no excuses," Felicity says.

You put the phone down and there's still no reply from Freddie. You cook your favourite and most complicated curry recipe, the one you never have time to cook because you're always too exhausted from work, although by the time it's done it's getting late.

You eat it in front of a sappy romantic comedy that's on the T.V. and go to bed without any reply from him.

*

When you wake up, he's sent you a message. It came through at six, and you think it must be his only 'me time'. Maybe workaholic wasn't an exaggeration.

"Sorry about the delay, hectic at work. Saturday is good. Choose a time and place and I'll see you there."

You sigh with relief that he's accepted, but now you have a new anxiety; where to suggest.

"Meet you at Movida Next Door at 8 p.m. I've booked." You send your reply while you're having lunch with Felicity. You needed to get her advice on venues.

"It's absolutely the place to be," she'd said, when you asked her for a dinner suggestion. "Eric took me there the other night and I ate so much I nearly exploded."

As Saturday evening looms, you realise you can't wear the same purple dress, although it would be perfect. You spend an hour choosing exactly the right combination of tops and slim fitting pants before jumping in a taxi to the restaurant because you're running late.

"Be there soon. Running late, sorry. Booking is in my name. x"

You've typed and sent the kiss before you can stop yourself.

Oh God, I've overdone it, he's going to leave before I even there, you think. As you step out of the cab you take five deep breaths, trying to calm the tremors in your hands.

I can do this. He's very nice, and he likes me, it will be fine, you repeat over and over to yourself. You don't really believe it but the breathing has helped you to settle.

Freddie is already seated at the table and he waves to you as he sees you arrive. He's wearing an incredibly dapper black suit, white shirt and thin black tie. It looks like the suit has been tailored and you think this is probably his very best outfit. You smile at the effort he's put in.

"Goodness, you scrub up well," you say as you lean over to kiss his cheek.

"As do you. Wow!" He waves his hands at your ensemble.

You order tapas and eat with your hands. As you reach for items of food your hand keeps brushing Freddie's. Every time a little thrill of electricity rushes through you.

He insists on paying again. "You're the one who's between jobs, remember?"

"I'm not broke," you say. "But you make a good point."

When you leave the restaurant and get out on the street you both stand silently.

"You're really cute," you blurt out as he says "Should we get another drink?" at the same time.

"Sorry, you go."

"I said, you're really cute," you say, your face flushing.

"I thought so." He looks serious for a moment then takes a half-step forward and lowering his lips to yours.

The electricity you felt from touching his hands is nothing compared to his kiss. Your legs start to go numb and you worry you might fall. He wraps his arms around you. They're firm and strong, and you feel safe.

He pulls away and breathes heavily, as though he's just run up a flight of stairs. You up look at his face, he is looking over your head down Flinders Street.

"What do we do now?" you ask, after he's been silent for a long time.

"I don't know. I... what do you want to do?"

"I mean, we could go find somewhere to get another drink. If you want." You feel shy and unsure.

"Yeah we could do that." He doesn't sound convinced.

"Or, uh, we could, uh, have a drink at my house?"

He drags his eyes away from the traffic and turns his intense gaze on you. He waits a beat, looking into your eyes, before a massive grin breaks through. "That sounds much better."

You take his hand and jump into the next taxi back to your house.

You win! You lost your job but you got a nice man.

C1.1.3 O2 You chose to take Felicity to the meeting …

As soon as you get off the phone from Joseph you call Felicity. You can feel tears threatening, but you push them down, you need to get through this phone call.

"Hi Soph," Felicity says, you can hear the smile in her voice.

"Hi," you croak.

"Are you okay?"

As soon as she asks, the control you had cracks. You start to sob, taking huge, shaking gulps of air as you try to speak.

"Nooooooo."

"What happened? Where are you?"

"Sorry, I…' You sniff and try talk normally. "Work. Work called. They want me to come to…a meeting. This afternoon. At two. I can bring someone. Can you come?"

"I can't, I'm at work…" Felicity hesitates. "No, fuck it. Of course I'll come. Give me a few minutes to rearrange some stuff. I'll call you back alright?"

"Alright."

"It'll be okay. Just, hang in there." She hangs up and you feel very alone. You look around your empty bedroom; your bed is strewn with chip crumbs and your head throbbing from too much wine. *What a mess*, you think.

Fleur Blüm

You lie back down and take stock. You opened an email that was sent to you in error, you probably shouldn't have, but it isn't entirely your fault. You believed that you had found something in the employee details that you shouldn't have been reading that were irregular at best and fraudulent at worst. You approached Calvin, someone you believed would clear up any misconceptions. You had thought you were pretty subtle about it, but instead, Calvin has now thrown allegations of sexual harassment at you.

Never in a million years would you have expected that to be the outcome. You wanted it to be all in your imagination, but now that you're getting dragged through this complaint process, there must be something else going on.

Now that you've accepted you're being set up, you have to work out what you'll do about it.

Cleared the arvo. Where is the meeting? Felicity texts. You reply with the address and start getting yourself ready.

The first thing is to get rid of your headache, you need to be thinking clearly. You get up and drink a full litre of water along with two paracetamol tablets.

The state of your bedroom reflects the state of your mind, so you tidy all the crumbs off the bed and put away all the clothes you've strewn around. Calm starts to come over you as everything is put in its proper place and the paracetamol kicks in.

When you arrive at the lawyers' offices in Collins Street fifteen minutes early, Felicity is already in the

65

ground floor foyer pacing up and down in ridiculously high heels.

"What have they told you about the meeting?" she asks as she gives you a tight hug.

"Almost nothing. They said they couldn't discuss it over the phone. He said it was preliminary, but we're in a lawyers' office."

"It doesn't bode well," Felicity agrees.

You take a quick nervous bathroom break and head up to the seventeenth floor. The lift ride up is silent, but Felicity reaches over and squeezes your hand briefly.

You look at her and smile. "Thank you for coming," you say.

Felicity doesn't have time to say anything as the lift dings and the doors slide silently open. Joseph is there to meet you as you step out.

"Sophie. Hi. Thanks so much for coming in," he says. You extend your hand to shake his and he hesitates slightly before taking it. You feel your hackles rising already.

"I felt I couldn't refuse," you say and Joseph drops your hand. "This is my support person, Felicity Baldwin. This is Joseph Sargeant, from HR."

Joseph leads you through to a conference room with frosted windows, probably to ensure privacy but you feel cut off from the world. In the room is a large dark wood conference table, its surface polished to a mirror-like shine. There are ten high-backed, black chairs around it and a jug of water and four glasses on the tabletop.

As you enter the room, you see that Joseph has brought someone too; an extremely well dressed and severe-looking woman in her late forties is already seated. Her salt and pepper hair is drawn back from her face in a bun so tight it pulls up the skin on her forehead.

"This is Germaine Spitznogle, she works here at the firm. She'll be taking notes."

You look over to Felicity before taking a seat at the table facing out the huge plate glass windows that look out over the stupid Ferris wheel down in the Docklands as well as pendulous, grey clouds.

"Before we begin, I need to go over some preliminary guidelines," Joseph says, as he sits next to Germaine. She has a sheaf of papers in front of her and you wish you'd brought something to take notes on.

"Sophie, you don't have to do or say anything but we would like to hear what you have to say about the matters in question. Felicity, you are here purely as a support person and witness for Sophie, you are not entitled to speak on her behalf. You may take notes."

Felicity glares at him, opens her mouth to say something but closes it again. She didn't bring anything to write on either.

Joseph lays out Calvin's complaint for you and Felicity. You both sit silently as he tells you about emails between you and Calvin, pornographic photos you've been sending as internal memos, and various conversations in which you have propositioned Calvin.

Once you're sure he's finished telling you the lies that he's been fed you stop to take a deep breath.

"Can I see the emails?" you ask.

"Uh," Joseph frowns and looks to Germaine who merely nods.

"Well, um, yes, I don't have them with me, but um, we can provide you with copies."

"Odd that you wouldn't have brought them to this meeting," you say. "And the pornographic material. I want copies of that too." You're surprised by how calm your voice seems. Again, Joseph looks to Germaine, who nods.

"I'll need some time to look over the materials, once I have them. What are the next steps? What happens now?" you ask.

"We were rather hoping that you would be able to respond in this meeting," Joseph says, his apple-cheeks reddening. "But, of course, you don't have to."

"There is a lot there to respond to. I'd prefer to have time to think about it." Your hands are clasped together so tightly that your fingers are turning white. "You'll have to send them to my personal email address, as I am not permitted to access my company one. I assume you have it?"

"Perhaps you should give it to me again, just in case." Joseph says, he doesn't look you in the eye. "Right. Once we have your response we'll determine whether sexual harassment has in fact occurred, and then we'll work out what appropriate disciplinary action can be taken," he continues.

"What might that involve?"

"Well, it might mean counselling or mediation, or it might go to termination of your employment."

"I see. And if the allegations are," you hesitate, "not found to be true?"

Joseph doesn't say anything.

"If they are proven to be spurious, then disciplinary action may be brought against the complainant," Germaine says in a voice as severe as her face.

"I see," you say again.

Nobody speaks and you decide not to be the first to say something.

"Thank you for coming in, Sophie, I think that's everything for today," Joseph says finally.

You stand up and walk out to the lifts with Felicity. She looks at you and you shake your head. The two of you remain silent until you step outside building when she turns to you, her face pale with anxiety.

"What the fuck was that?" she asks quietly.

"I've been set up. Let's get a coffee."

You walk towards the nearest coffee shop; you don't want to discuss anything in the street. You order a coffee for each of you and only when it sits in front of you do you start to explain your suspicions. Felicity listens silently, her mouth pressed into a thin line.

"What are you gonna do?"

"I don't know." You lip starts to tremble and you force the tears back. "Thank you for today."

"What else would I do, babe?" She squeezes your hand again.

"Do you think I need a lawyer?"

"Yeah, I think you probably should."

You smile grimly. "You're right."

Felicity heads back to work for a couple of hours as you go home. You pull out your phone and look for employment lawyers. It will be expensive but there's a principle at stake that's worth pursuing.

Sophie's Path

You find a firm that looks like they have good reviews online, and you make quick call. The receptionist explains that one of the lawyers will call you back, before giving you a rundown of the fee structure.

You make your way home, there's no point waiting around for the lawyer to call. You probably won't be able to do anything much until you have the copies of the materials from Joseph.

The next day, you get a call, you're still in bed looking through Face book on your phone.

"Hello, Sophie, this is Angus Strong, from Morris Blainbury. I understand that you're in a situation where you'd like our advice."

You go over the story again, trying to keep it succinct, given how much this is costing you. He listens without interrupting you.

"If the allegations are false, you need to refute them, but it's a very dangerous position to be in," he says when you finish.

"What are you advising? That I quit? They're defrauding the company of tens of thousands of dollars a year. I mean, that's what this is all about, that unknown employee in the spreadsheet."

"I understand that. I don't think it's a good idea to bring that up just now. Respond to the complaint in hand first."

CHOOSE:

If you decide to take the lawyer's advice, go to p 72.

If you decide to ignore the lawyer's advice, go to p 77.

C1.1.4 O1 You chose to take the lawyer's advice…

"Alright, if you think that's best. But I won't let myself be steamrolled by a false accusation."

"No one wants you to get the blame for something you didn't do. Once we've established your innocence, we can raise your concerns about fraudulent activity. Okay? Leave it with me."

"Thank you," you say, feeling like you're already defeated.

"When you get those emails etc., forward them to me." He gives you an email address, "I'll be in touch when I find something." He hangs up.

The process takes several more weeks, waiting for Joseph to send you the emails, and then for the lawyer Angus to look over them. You are not allowed to return to the office. The company continues to pay your salary, but you're at a loss as to what to do with your time.

You spend a lot of time exercising; you clean out your wardrobe, kitchen cupboards, and storage space. You start teaching yourself how to make jams and preserves. You buy six adult colouring books. But you still feel fundamentally empty and increasingly lost without work in your life.

For the first two weeks you feel like you need to stay faithful to the company. By the third week you start applying for new jobs.

It makes you sad to think of leaving the company, up until now they'd been excellent employers. If they can't see through Calvin's lies, even if they don't fire you, you can't continue to work there.

The longer it goes on, the less inclined you are to go back into the office. People will have heard about why you're not in by now and you can't help thinking what they'll say even if you come back.

Your phone rings and it's the lawyer, Angus Strong.

"Hi," you can't manage to put much energy into your voice.

"I have news. Good news. Are you free to talk?"

You laugh. "Yes, I'm just at home trying to work out what I'm doing with my life."

"Ah, I see. Well, I was reading over some of the emails that were allegedly sent from your address and I've noticed a few inconsistencies. Not in the first sections but when there's an email trail, they get, weird. Corrupt or something. I'm having one of our tech guys look at it but I think it's proof that the emails are false, which then brings into question the entire claim."

"Right." You know that it's good news, but after six weeks of exile you're bitter and resentful. You're also starting to lose hope.

"I know it's been a hard process for you. I suppose they considered the claim to be quite serious and didn't expect you to refute it. Anyway, I think we can get this cleared up by the end of next week."

You and Angus are called into another meeting in the lawyers' office with Joseph and Germaine the following Friday. Angus seems to think it's a good sign.

"Most people won't fire you on a Friday," he says as you walk in.

"Why not?"

"Suicide. There's evidence that firing people on a Friday doubles the chances they'll kill themselves." He smiles reassuringly, but you don't feel any better.

The four of you sit around the mirror-like board table.

"Thank you for coming in again, Sophie," Joseph says.

You don't say anything.

"We've been given some interesting material from Angus,." Joseph always addresses you, although since you engaged the lawyer, Angus has been answering on your behalf.

"About the emails on which the claims against you have been heavily based. He's been able to demonstrate that the emails have been altered from their original state," he continues. There is a pause and you suppose you should acknowledge him.

"I see," you say.

"Yes. So we looked into the legislative hold, that's a store of all emails that come into and go out of the company, I hadn't been aware we had one before Angus suggested we look in it. We were able to determine that these emails were changed after you sent them, and that in fact, you did not send the harassing content. The emails have been doctored, we suspect by Calvin."

"Right," you say. You keep your responses minimal, as Angus advised, until they say they're dropping the claim.

"Given that the emails were falsified, we have difficulty believing that the other claims were genuine. We're confident that you did not act inappropriately and that Calvin, for reasons which are still unclear, has fabricated the complaint."

"I did say I didn't do it." You glare at Joseph when you speak. "Six weeks ago."

"That's it then, the complaint is found to be unsubstantiated. You're welcome back to the office tomorrow." Joseph smiles at you. You feel your stomach tighten and you feel a bit sick.

You turn to Angus, who nods and turns back to Joseph.

"Now that Sophie has been cleared of theses vexatious and false allegations, there are a few other matters. Firstly, we'll be filing a counter-complaint against Calvin for dragging Sophie through this three-ring circus. Since you have shown that the emails are in fact fraudulent, we expect him to be disciplined swiftly."

"Yes, well, of course Sophie has every right to make a complaint." Joseph is fidgeting with his pen.

"There is also another matter, which my client was hesitant to bring up while the harassment complaint was still being investigated. That is, she has reason to believe there are irregularities in the payroll. She believes this is the reason the complaint of sexual harassment was fabricated against her in the first place."

Joseph opens and closes his mouth like a fish. "Irregularities in the payroll?" he says finally.

"Yes, I was mistakenly sent an email from Emily which I had opened before I realised it was not addressed to me. There was an attachment containing a list of all employees along with their salaries and other personal details. I opened the attachment, something I admit I should not have done, but I noticed someone who is not, to my knowledge, an employee, nor has this person ever been an employee. I raised this issue with Calvin, and three days later he made his complaint against me."

"We're happy to provide you with anything you need in this matter, however, since you have access, have had access to Sophie's emails, and the legislative hold, for this whole period, you may as well look for yourself. The email is from Emily Sidero," Angus says.

You return to the office the following Monday and notice it's now Calvin and Emily's desks that are vacant.

"They're being investigated. What a mess!" Candace says when you ask her where they are.

"I'm so sorry about this whole thing. It's been a complete disaster since you've been gone. I haven't been able to call you. I never believed you'd do anything like this and I'm so glad you're back." Candace is gushing.

"It's so nice to hear you say that," you say, feeling your face flush with emotion.

You've successfully resolved the fraud and kept your job. Calvin and Emily are fired and charged with embezzling funds.

The end.

C1.1.4 O2 You chose to ignore the lawyer's advice…

"I can't just sit here and get the blame for something I didn't do because they're hiding the fact they're ripping the company off! I have to say something."

"I would strenuously advise against that," your lawyer says.

"I don't want to hear what you advise right now."

You hang up on him and immediately dial Aubrey Drake, the CEO.

"Aubrey speaking," he sounds flustered.

"Hi, it's Sophie Faithful. I need to tell you about something which I think—"

"Sophie? I've been told not to take your calls right now. I'll to put you through to Joseph."

"I don't want to talk to that jackass." You know you sound unreasonable.

"I'm just putting you through."

"No!" you say, but all you hear is hold music. You briefly consider calling Aubrey back, but he won't listen, if he even answers.

"Hello, this is Joseph."

"Yeah, it's Sophie. I was just trying to have a private conversation with Aubrey when he transferred me to you."

"Yes, that's the procedure. If you need to speak with anyone in the company, you can talk directly to me."

"Right. This whole thing is just ridiculous. I never fucking harassed Calvin. He's making it up, and I'll tell you why–"

"Sophie, please let's keep things professional," Joseph says in his infuriatingly calm voice.

"He's fabricated a case against me because he and Emily Sidero, from Finance, have been skimming money from the company."

"That's quite a serious thing to say. Are you sure you want to make that statement?"

"Yes, I'm sure! This whole thing is an attempt to discredit me so that when I bring this to you you'll believe them and not me."

Joseph says nothing.

"If you're not even going to hear me out then I may as well just fucking quit now and be done with it."

"If you feel like you no longer wish to work here, we can't stop you from leaving."

"You'd love that, wouldn't you? You could just pin the blame on me and I would just disappear…" You're panting, you don't think you've ever been this angry before.

"I would never force you to resign, obviously that isn't what we're aiming for, but it is a very difficult situation you're making it worse for yourself by coming to me with these ridiculous claims."

You want to scream that you have proof, but of course you don't have access to your emails. You bite the inside of your cheek until the urge subsides.

Fleur Blüm

"So, for the sake of argument. If I were to resign now, would the company give me a good reference?"

"We would be able to give you a statement of service. As for your manager, that's entirely at her discretion. The fact that this matter is not resolved one way or the other would mean that we wouldn't be able to say anything about it."

"Right. Goodbye then."

You hang up the phone, with a sigh. You feel like you've been pushed into resigning from a job you love. Joseph didn't seem to give any reasons to stay; you think it would be easier for him if you were gone.

Maybe it's best. Have a fresh start and leave Emily and Calvin to lie in the bed they've made for themselves. You run your hands over your face and wish your temper hadn't gotten the better of you.

It takes you an hour to write a letter of resignation and send it by email to Candace and Aubrey, with a copy to Joseph.

At least I don't have to deal with going through with the investigation, you think. It feels like you've failed.

You have lost your job and did not resolve
the fraud. Go back and try again.

C1.1 O2 You chose to push the meet and greet to tomorrow....

You do a quick mental calculation.

"I really don't think I can make it there and back today. Can I do it first thing in the morning?"

Candace screws up her face.

"Honestly with getting over there and back it would hardly be worth going at all, and I have to be back here for a four o'clock meeting. I can be there at nine tomorrow and spend the whole morning with them..."

Candace doesn't seem impressed.

"Okay, give me Jeremy's number and I'll introduce myself over the phone now. It's the best I can do," you say.

"Fine," she says with a loud sigh.

When you arrive back at your desk you see that Calvin's office door is open and both he and Emily are not in the office. With this new client you can't waste time watching Emily.

Fifteen minutes before the four o'clock meeting, the client calls to cancel.

"Of course, that's fine," you say down the phone, silently pressing your nails into your palms in frustration.

I should have gone to the new client, you think. You hang up the phone and see that Calvin and Emily are still out.

What could they be doing? Neither has any client facing duties, they're almost always at their desks. Emily does something in Finance and Calvin does Payroll

It's also possible that whatever they're doing, they're doing it separately. But then what was the closed door about?

You shake your head and stand up, stretching your arms up towards the ceiling and twisting at the waist. You walk over to Candace's office.

"Coffee, Candace?" you ask, as you lean your head around her door.

You see she's on a call, but she hears your question, and rolls her eyes at the phone. With her free hand she picks up her mostly empty coffee cup and waves it at you.

You take the cup and she moves her mouth to say thank-you as you retreat towards the kitchen.

Candace's cup has about half an inch of scungy coffee in the bottom of it. She tends to get caught up in her work and things like putting her cup in the dishwasher become a low-level priority. You recall the time you found her with four or five cups collected on her desk.

You spot Jude in the kitchen and you nod to him as you approach.

"How's things?" he asks.

"I just had a really frustrating phone call and needed to get up for a while. Thought I'd make Candace a coffee while I'm up. She's really under the pump."

"I figured as much from that presentation you did in the meeting today. Isn't that her job?"

You hesitate, washing out the coffee cups before answering.

"I suppose so. It's my job, too. She had to be out on site with a client, so I was happy to do it for her." You don't know Jude that well, you get the sense he's fishing for something.

"When you put it like that..." he trails off.

You wait for him to say something else, running your eyes over the office kitchen with its grey cupboards, grey countertops, generic white fridge and darker grey linoleum floor. You sigh. "How's working for Max going?" you ask.

Jude moved into the team you used to work in a month or so after you left. He hadn't been with the company long before that either. He looks about the same age as you, or possibly a little younger. His strong features always look angry, and his dark hair is always overly styled so that it doesn't move, but despite that he's quite handsome.

"He certainly has a…an unusual management style." He smiles at you. When he smiles you feel your face becoming hot; it feels like he's about to eat you and you like it.

You look down at the cups in your hands smiling. "He does, but he has your best interests at heart and knows his stuff. It took me a while to get used to it," you say.

Jude sips his coffee, his eyes fixed on a point in the middle distance.

CHOOSE:

If you stay and chat more with Jude, go to <u>p 84.</u>

If you go back to your desk, go to <u>p 140.</u>

C1.1.1 O1 You chose to stay to chat more with Jude...

"Are you alright?" you ask, feeling the silence stretch out.

"Hmm? Sorry, miles away." He smiles at you again, and the heat in your cheeks spreads down your neck.

"I was just wondering, I know I'm only fairly new, but was there something going on with Finance this morning in the meeting?" Jude asks, shifting his weight onto his other foot.

"Can you be more specific?" You immediately think of Calvin and Emily whispering. You've been telling yourself all afternoon that you were being paranoid, maybe it wasn't just you.

"I don't wanna start any rumours or anything, but," he lifts his eyes to yours briefly, "Emily and that guy from Payroll, they seemed...what was all the whispering about?"

You press your lips together firmly and stir sugar into Candace's coffee. "I don't know, is the honest answer. I clocked it too and I didn't know what to make of it. They went straight into Calvin's office, he's the guy from Payroll, after the meeting. I thought I was just being paranoid."

It feels like a massive weight has been lifted from your shoulders once you say it aloud.

"Ah," Jude says.

You wonder if you should give him some more background, to see if he'll share his thoughts with you if you go first.

"I was hesitant because, well, Emily and I don't really get on…she's not really my type. Very ambitious, she puts herself before anything else. I have concerns about the way she gets results. Nothing concrete of course, just a feeling. From her I would have expected whispering and secret meetings, but Calvin always seemed so…" You struggle to find the right word.

"Straight forward?" Jude offers.

"Yeah, I guess so." You glance at your coffees sitting on the bench between you.

"As I say, I don't know much about Calvin, but what you've said about Emily is true enough. I know her through family friends, she recommended I apply here actually, and she's certainly determined. I've always admired it about her, but I can imagine there are a few toes she's stepped on along the way."

You're surprised that anyone would admire Emily, but you file that away for later. As much as you might be tempted to do so you know you shouldn't trust Jude too quickly.

"I'm sure there have been." You laugh, but it sounds forced. "I'd better get back to my desk."

"Yeah, me too, I umm—" he breaks off and looks uncomfortable.

"You umm?" you say.

"Sorry, I was wondering if I could make a time to pick your brains, this project Max has me working on, I, well I think I'm going about it all wrong. It seems to be very hard and I'm sure there's an easier way it could be done if I could just work out what it is!"

You laugh genuinely, releasing the tension you didn't realise you were holding. This must be what he was reluctant to ask you about, and it explains the awkwardness of the meeting.

"Of course! Happy to help, I used to do your job so, anytime. Tomorrow after lunch might work?"

"Great, I'll get my head in order and work out exactly what I need to know."

Jude walks away with a slight bounce in his step. You pick up the two coffees and head back through the open plan section towards Candace's office.

You can't knock on Candace's door as you go in with both hands full. You gently push her door open ahead of you with your toe. Candace is on the phone looking a little tight and anxious. She waves you in and indicates for you to have a seat.

"Yes, okay, I'll get onto that and have recommendations for by the end of next week." She hangs up the phone and reaches for the coffee you've placed on her desk.

"You're a lifesaver, truly!" she says before taking a sip.

"I do my best."

"That was Aubrey. He's just met with a hotel client who wants to open a new office in Mackay."

"Oh, right," you say.

"Yeah, he's really thrown me for a loop, you know. He wants someone to go up, with the client, and help set up the new office and try to get us other clients in the area at the same time."

"Like create a new branch? Sounds like hard work but a great opportunity…"

"It is, but Aubrey wants to take someone from my team. I'm just feeling a bit overwhelmed at the idea of losing someone right now. With everything that's been going on, the workload and all the rest of it, it's the last thing I need." She sighs and has another sip of her coffee.

"I'm sure Aubrey will let you replace the person he's taking. But then you still have to recruit and that's a pain." You're not sure what you can do; whether you should try to comfort Candace or to offer solutions.

"Yes. He will," she says finally. "Your name came up."

"My name?" you say, somewhat surprised.

"Yeah, he was particularly pleased with your presentation this morning in the meeting. I guess you've been making an impression lately. You know you're my star, it's not really a surprise that other people have noticed it too."

"Uh, thanks."

"Anyway, thanks for the coffee. I better get cracking. I'm going to write up Aubrey's proposal and send it out to everyone in the team. Then, if people are interested they can apply for the new role and I'll send Aubrey my top picks of the volunteers assuming there are any." Candace looks down at her desk and seems tired.

"You're great at spinning the good out of any situation. If your email is enticing, people will be jumping at the chance to live in Mackay for a bit. How long did you say?"

"Six months, at least, possibly more depending on how successful the project is."

"Six months is a good length."

You stand up to leave Candace's office and your mind is whirling with possibilities. When you log back into your computer you find that Jude has sent you a meeting invitation for Friday morning.

Between Jude, Calvin and Emily, this new client, and the possibility of work in Mackay, your stable work world seems to have been completely turned upside down.

On Friday morning you head into one of the small meeting rooms and see that Jude is already there with his laptop on the pine-veneer meeting table.

"I've been able to spend some time figuring out exactly what I need your help with. Pull up a chair and I'll show you where I'm running into trouble generating these reports."

The chairs are black bucket-style chairs, with the back and seat moulded from a single piece of MDF. The boardrooms have executive chairs with wheels but these small meeting rooms have the cheaper non-wheel variety.

At least we shouldn't take too long, you think as you sit down.

You spend a little over an hour going through various questions Jude has about how to manipulate the data before he finally leans back. "I think I have it under control now."

"No worries at all. If that's everything I have this new client that's taking up all my time. You're welcome to come back to me if you run into any trouble though."

As you start to get up Jude reaches out and puts his hand on your arm.

"I...wanted to talk to you about something else actually," he says.

"Okay," you say, sitting down again.

"You know how we mentioned Calvin and Emily the other day? Well I got an email the other day from Emily, I don't think it was supposed to go to me, it was talking about a guy called John Smith and his salary and stuff." He looks out through the glass wall of the meeting room, "I don't know any employees call John Smith, do you?

"I haven't heard of a John Smith, but that doesn't necessarily mean he doesn't work here. I mean, Emily does work in Finance, she's got access to the accounts and to payroll, so..." You are trying not to say anything to agree with Jude outright, but it does sound quite fishy.

"Yeah, you're probably right." Jude looks down at his lap, he looks flat, disappointed.

"I mean, keep an eye on it, you know, for the future, but I don't think anything will come of it." You put your hand on his shoulder to comfort him and you're surprised by how much you enjoy the feeling of his warm skin through his shirt.

"Thanks. I just get a bad feeling. At least now I've told someone." He smiles weakly and you wish you could do something to cheer him up.

You still have your hand on his shoulder and you start to gently move it across the pale-blue fabric.

"Are you doing anything good after work?" you say, trying to steer the conversation away from conspiracy theories about Emily and Calvin.

"No, not tonight, but I'm going to a warehouse party down the Docklands tomorrow. There's going to be some epic DJs there. You?" he asks.

"Really? I think I might be going to the same party with my bestie, Felicity." You aren't sure whether you should invite Jude to come with you, or to meet you there, or whether to mention that you might bump into each other. You're suddenly anxious about overstepping friendly work colleague boundaries even as your hand is caressing his shoulder.

"Amazing! I'm sure we'll run into each other. Although, if you like, we could eat somewhere first and then we wouldn't have to arrive alone..." he says, before a small frown appears on his face. "Unless of course you're already going with someone. Shit, sorry, I made that awkward didn't I?"

You laugh, reluctantly removing your hand from his shoulder. You can still feel the residual warmth. "No, I'm not arriving with anyone, and you didn't make it awkward. I'd be happy to meet you for food somewhere. I don't know anywhere down that end of town though."

"No, neither do I really. I'll have a bit of a look online this afternoon. I'll email you or maybe it's better if I text you?" he says.

As you sit back at your desk it occurs to you that Jude has just very smoothly gotten your personal phone number. Not that it's a particular secret, but if he were interested in something more than a purely work relationship, he was certainly progressing nicely. You smile to yourself and wonder if it would really be that bad to date a colleague.

Having dinner with guy from work, see you at the gig, you text Felicity as you head out the door a little after seven on Saturday night.

Jude found a pub not far from the venue which apparently has reputable steaks. You don't often eat steak, but when you do, you like it to be good quality.

Guy from work? Is this new? Is this a thing? Bring him over when you get to gig!! Felicity texts back.

The pub is in a little out of the way corner of the Docklands overlooking the water. No matter how many times you come down this way you can't get used to the eerie stillness of it. There never seem to be any people around and you feel decidedly unsafe walking under the yellow light of the sodium streetlamps.

When you walk into the pub Jude is already there. He's loitering at the bar chatting to the staff about the AFL football playing on the big screen. The place, O'Malley's, has the feel of an Irish theme pub; the carpet is green and the bar is decorated with soccer paraphernalia and shamrocks. It's huge, but not very full, adding to the feeling that you're not quite safe.

"Are your team playing?" you ask as you walk up beside him. He jumps, startled.

"Jeez! I didn't see you come in!" He looks a little wild-eyed, but since he's smiling you suspect he's only half-serious.

"Sorry, I'll wear a bell next time." You grin back at him.

"What're you drinking?"

"Umm, white wine to start, I think," you say, looking at the half empty pint of beer in his hand. He's got a bit of a head start, but perhaps he's nervous, you think. It occurs to you that Jude might be more than a year or two younger than you. The idea of being the older woman added to the fact that he's a work colleague make this a liaison with just enough potential for disaster to make it exciting.

You and Jude both order the steak, you like yours rare, he orders medium. When they arrive they're delicious, tender and flavourful.

"I wouldn't have expected the steaks here to be so good!" you say.

"I have to admit I'm pleasantly surprised too. I just Googled the place and thought I'd give it a whirl. I've not been here before. I don't tend to spend much time in the Docklands."

"They keep trying to get people down here, but it still always feels creepy to me," you say before you can stop yourself. Surely he'll think you're bonkers if you go on about it being creepy.

He shrugs. "Maybe it's because there's nothing on the side where the water is, it feels emptier than it is."

You glance at the time. "We have time for another drink before we go over. Shall I go up this time?"

So far Jude has bought all the drinks and you're starting to feel uncomfortably like this is a date. If he lets you buy this round you hope that is an indication of friendship level rather than relationship level expectations.

"Yes, alright, I'll have a pint of cider, thanks!" he says cheerfully.

At the bar, you feel empty; you must have wanted this to be a date.

So what are you going to do about it? You think to yourself. You text Felicity while you're waiting for the barman to return with your drinks.

I think I like guy from work, I think I want this to be a thing. You have to help.

Roger roger. Mission accepted, she texts back within a minute.

You're surprised by how quickly she replied. Either she's on the way to the venue now, or it's really boring. She wouldn't be sitting on her phone if it was pumping.

When you and Jude have finished your drinks you walk over to the venue. It's not far from the pub but there's a stiff, cold breeze coming across the water making it feel further away.

"It's a bit nippy, eh?" Jude says, looking over to see you hunched into your jacket.

"It's not too bad, but I've dressed for inside, not for outside," you laugh, although it sounds strained.

"Yeah, you'll warm up when we get inside." He winks at you and you feel something stirring inside you.

Before you can think about that wink too long you're being moved along into the massive building. The loud, throbbing techno music was clearly audible from outside and once you step into the main hall it's so loud you feel like the music is touching you. It's vibrating through your feet and thrumming in your chest. You close your eyes and enjoy the feeling of the sound caressing you, which seems a little weird given the fast techno beat.

The venue is a converted warehouse; it has high ceilings and you can see silver pipes running along the rafters. They must be heating or cooling, you think. The floors are bare concrete, but in one corner an area has been set up around bar which has astro-turf and a white picket fence.

"I need to find my friend, then we need to get another drink," you say, leaning close to Jude's ear to be heard over the music.

He nods and gestures with a sweep of his arm that he will follow your lead.

You find Felicity tucked away in one of the chill out rooms, a small area off the main room with a few vinyl-covered couches. The couches are looking a bit worse for wear even with the low lighting. She jumps up to greet you as soon as you come close.

"Is this him?" she asks as she hugs you.

"Yes, this is Jude. He does my old job with Max."

"He's pretty cute, if a little young. You cougar!"

"Now that we've found you, we need more drinks," you say. The music is not as loud in this section where it spills into the room from the main stage through the open doorway and vibrates through the thin wall panels.

"Oh, let me introduce Eric." Felicity waves over a very tall, blond, man. His curly hair reminds you of a renaissance cherub and his strong facial features are more like a Viking.

"And this is Eric's friend, Tom," she adds, waving to a brown-haired man who would probably look much more imposing if he weren't next to the Viking.

"Eric is just going to the bar, aren't you?" Felicity prods him.

As Eric walks off towards the bar, Felicity loops her arm through Jude's and leads him to one of the couches. You take a seat on a nearby couch, next to Tom, and try to hear what she's saying to Jude.

"So do you work with Felicity?" Tom asks, in a velvety-bass voice.

"No, I actually work in the same office as Jude. I know Felicity from uni. What about you, where do you know Eric from?"

"Friend of a friend originally, I think." He smiles at you and shows off perfect straight white teeth.

Your conversation with Tom is shallow, focusing on work and what's good on Netflix recently. When Eric returns with the drinks he joins you and Tom. Felicity is still talking to Jude, their heads hovering close together.

It's Eric's turn now to ask how you know Felicity, what you do for work, and what your other plans are for rest of the weekend. He keeps looking at the other two when he thinks you aren't looking.

"Should we break them up do you think?" you say, just as Eric is distracted from his story for the seventh time to look longingly at Felicity.

"Pardon?" Eric replies.

"Well, you look like you want to talk to Flick, and I was hoping to get to know Jude better, so perhaps we should arrange a swap." You wink at him and he seems to catch your meaning.

"Give him up," you say into Felicity's ear, gently pulling her arm toward the other couch. She offers no resistance and moves over between Eric and Tom. She has the look of a cat purring.

"What was that all about? It must have been terribly interesting to occupy her like that."

"I could tell you, but then I'd have to kill you," Jude replies, winking.

Eventually you decide to move into the main stage room. You conversation with Jude is stilted trying to compete with the music and Felicity and Eric have started snogging on the couch. When you get up Tom comes with you.

Jude takes your hand as you walk through the crowded room, there are a lot more people here now and the main room is buzzing. The three of you find a good spot in the crowd, in front of the stage but about a third of the way back. Jude doesn't let go of your hand until a well-known banger comes on and everyone, including Jude, starts to jump up and down manically.

You're swept up in the music and when you finally realise how tired you are you see that it's late. Tom slipped off at some point earlier, though you didn't notice. You have a message from Felicity saying she's gone home with the Viking.

"I think I'm going to call it a night," you say.

"Really? I was just getting into it...I'll come with you." Jude looks at his watch. "Wow, I didn't realise it was that late! Time flies eh?"

Fleur Blüm

You thread your way through the crowd and out into
the street. You wave down the first taxi you see and
you're surprised when it stops for you.

"Can I give you a ride home?" Jude says, mock
gallantly.

CHOOSE:

If you go home with Jude, go to p 99.

If you go home alone, go to p 109.

C1.1.5 O1 You chose to go home with Jude…

"Why certainly, kind sir, that would be delightful," you say imitating his tone.

Jude jumps in the back of the taxi with you. "Your place or mine?" he whispers, putting his hand on your thigh.

You giggle. "Yours?"

"St Kilda, please, driver," he says and gives the cabbie the address.

You don't say anything the whole trip, not wanting to spoil the moment. Jude's hand remains on your thigh, you don't acknowledge it, but you don't push it away either. You enjoy the warm electricity you feel through your skirt and you can feel your arousal building. It's not far and the drive seems to be over in a moment.

Jude's place is an older apartment block just behind Acland Street, all curves and circles in typical art deco style. It's one bedroom, with what might be charitably called minimalist décor, or uncharitably called sparse. Everything inside is beige: the carpets, the walls, the couch, the bookshelf, the tiny kitchen, everything you see seems beige.

As soon as you and Jude are inside, Jude shuts the front door and wraps his arms around you kissing you deeply. Your handbag dangles from your hand as you are swept up in him. His arms are strong and his embrace is firm and comforting. You taste cider in his mouth and he smells a little like sweat, with his musky cologne over it.

You drop your bag and fling your arms around his neck, trying to get closer to him. He wraps his arm around your waist and lifts you off your feet. You break the kiss to squeal with excitement, you haven't been lifted like that for a long time.

Jude makes a sounds somewhere between a growl and a giggle and carries you into his bedroom, which you notice is also beige, before flinging you onto the bed. You land with your legs and arms flailing all over the place and sink into the gorgeous softness of his off-white bedding.

Jude grabs your feet and pulls off your ridiculously high heels; he pauses briefly to kiss the top of each foot. He takes your ankles and wraps them around him as he crawls onto the bed between your legs. You can feel the hardness of his erection pressing onto your groin. You can feel yourself twitching in response.

Now above you, Jude presses his body against yours, and kisses his way along your neck and into your cleavage. You bring your hands up to his head and bury your fingers in his luscious dark hair. You let out a little moan as he nuzzles his face between your breasts.

"You don't know how long I've wanted to do this," he says, his voice muffled by your clothing.

"Oh really?"

"Mmmmhmmmm," he says into your chest, his voice vibrating through you.

He reaches up under your skirt and pulls off your knickers. You feel exposed and try to draw your knees together, but Jude gently stops you, moving his face down towards your wet pussy.

Sophie's Path

It feels slightly strange to be still mostly clothed while Jude works between your legs, but it isn't long before you lose yourself in the sensation.

You are vaguely aware of the shuffling sounds of Jude removing his own clothes, and when you lift your head to look at him, he is wearing only tight boxers.

He looks at you, now kneeling on the bed, back between your legs. With one hand, he strokes his swollen cock through the boxers, you can see even under the fabric, that it is big and beautiful. In one swift movement he flips aside his boxers and lays himself between your legs. This time there is no fabric to disguise the heat between you.

"Yes?" He whispers, his breath hot on your ear.

"Yes! Yes, yes." You grip his hips and guide him into you, letting out a sigh of pleasure as he slides deeply in.

Jude moves slowly, you're sure he's taunting you on purpose.

"Oh God, faster!" You squeak.

"Mmmm, yes," he says, but doesn't change his pace.

"Turn over," he says, his voice deep and commanding. You lie face down on the bed and Jude reaches one hand around to run slippery circles over your clit as he slides himself inside.

You can feel your climax building and he finally starts to thrust faster and harder. You're helpless to stop yourself.

"I'm gonna cum," you say, just in time for shudders and ripples of orgasm wrack your body.

As your consciousness returns to the room you can hear Jude shuddering in response, his body curled around yours, twitching slightly. He rests his head on your shoulder, his breath and yours slowly returning to normal.

Jude rolls off you, pulling you with him so you're spooning.

"Thank you," he says finally.

"No, thank you," you reply, caressing the arm he still has wrapped around you.

*

You wake up in the grey early morning light still wearing your party dress to find Jude is gone. You're surprised you could have fallen asleep so easily in a strange house still dressed. You hear water running in the bathroom, and you turn your head to take in Jude's bedroom in the light. As soon as you move daggers of pain behind your eyes remind you how much you drank last night and you groan.

The water stops and Jude comes out wrapped in a towel but still wet and glistening. His body is toned without being huge; he would have what might be described as wiry strength rather than brute strength. With the glow of the water and the morning light he looks delicious.

"Morning, sleepy," he says, coming over to kiss your forehead.

"God, I must look like a train wreck, I'm sure my makeup's everywhere," you protest.

"You look like you've had a good time. I will take some of the blame for the smeared makeup." He winks. "I'm going to make something to eat, if you want a shower."

"Yes, that would be good." You struggle out of the bed and into the bathroom.

The hot water feels amazing on your skin, you let it run over you, cascading through your hair and washing away the residues of last night.

When you step out of the cubicle and start to dry yourself, you notice that Jude is standing at the door, still wearing a towel. He lets it drop and he reaches for you.

"I got distracted," he says, walking you back to the bed.

You explore each other more calmly this time, the urgency of the first time replaced by indulgence. When you're both sweaty and satiated, your belly rumbles loudly and you both laugh.

"Alright, alright, I will actually make food," Jude says, slapping your bottom playfully before he goes into the kitchen.

You and Jude decide not to mention your hook-up, or whatever it is, to people at work. *Best to see where it goes first,* you tell yourself.

The week at work is long and boring; your mind keeps wandering to Jude. Wondering what he's doing, or when you might be able to see him again. You text a couple of times a day, but make a point of not seeing one another at lunchtime or hanging around too much in the kitchen area.

"Have you given any thought to the Queensland job?" Candace asks you on Friday, "I need your application by the end of the day if you're going to apply."

"Yeah, I'm getting to it," you reply, distractedly. You dash away to the toilet, for what feels like the fiftieth time today, only to suffer through intense burning pain as you pee. You tried the alkalising sachets last night, and usually they clear up a urinary tract infection fairly quickly, but the pain isn't lessening. You're starting to worry it isn't just a UTI.

Back at your desk, you call the doctor across the road from your office and book yourself in. She can't see you for another hour, so you get started on the job application. If you get offered the placement and you and Jude have something worth staying for, you can always turn it down.

You become lost in writing your covering letter and updating your resume and when your computer jangles with the alert to go to the doctors you're caught by surprise.

"Back in half an hour. Maybe less. I'm doing the application now, I promise."

Candace merely nods as you hurry away.

The doctor is running fifteen minutes late, so you didn't need to rush.

"What seems to be the trouble?" she asks when you're sitting in a chair beside her desk.

"Uh, it's a little bit delicate...it burns when I pee." You can feel your face colouring.

"I see, and how long has this been going on?" The doctor continues in her same almost dreamy way.

"It started yesterday about lunch time."

"Right. Recent sexual activity?"

You breathe in sharply, her blunt question putting you more off balance. "Uh, yes, over the weekend."

"Male or female?"

"Male."

"Was it a new partner? Did you use condoms?"

103

You look away, staring at your shoes. "Yes, it was a new partner, and…the first time I was too drunk to remember the condoms and then it didn't seem like it was worth insisting."

"I see." She starts to type something into the computer.

"How long has it been since you had an STI screening? We don't have one on our system."

"This isn't my usual doctor. But umm, I don't remember."

The doctor explains that there are several possibilities for why you might be experiencing burning, some of which are sexually transmitted infections. She performs a Pap smear and a few other swab tests, and then asks you to pee into a cup, which is agonising.

"The results with take a few days, but we'll call you as soon as we hear anything."

You feel soiled, and stupid. You decide not to see Jude over the weekend, whatever the problem is, it will not be helped by more sex.

I can tell him I've got family stuff, you think.

Back at your desk you give your application a final read over and send it to Candace. Seeing as it's four o'clock on a Friday and you feel pretty depressed and fragile you ask if it's alright to head off a bit early.

"Of course, you've put in a lot of work this week. Take a nice weekend break and see you on Monday." Candace smiles at you, but she looks stressed and worried.

Hey sexy, I can't hang out this weekend, I'm feeling a bit under the weather and I have to do some family things, sorry. Maybe one night next week I can cook you dinner?

You feel cowardly hiding from Jude but if you got something from him last weekend the last thing you want to do is go back for more. Plus he'd probably be suspicious if you demanded protection now after neglecting it the last few times.

Oh baby! I'm sorry to hear that. You look after yourself and if you need me to bring you chicken soup or something, just hit me up. xxx Jude replies almost immediately.

By Sunday morning the burning has cleared itself up, and you have decided it must have been a UTI which just took a little longer to go away. Feeling suddenly horny you invite Jude over for dinner.

After falling into a frantic fuck when he arrived, you share a pizza before more sex. You fall asleep in each other's arms. In the morning, Jude convinces you, with very little effort, to have a quickly before he leaves early on Monday morning to get ready for work. You smile all day and think about whether maybe there is something in this. At work you and Jude are back to ignoring each other.

Candace asks you into her office first thing on Tuesday. "I bet you can guess what this is about," she starts, smiling tightly.

"The Mackay job?"

"Yes, Aubrey and I went through the applications last night and, as I suspected, you were the stand out from the group. We've prepared a position description and a letter outlining the exact package, salary and incentives, we're offering. I thought you could take these with you and let me know tomorrow. Aubrey wants to announce it at the meeting."

"Of course he does." You don't say it in a mean-spirited way, but Aubrey can be quite bull-headed when he chooses to be.

"I have to get to some stuff on my emails, so unless you have any pressing questions?" Candace says, and you know the meeting is over.

"Not at the moment. I'll have a read and let you know if I need any clarification," you say, taking the pile of papers and heading back to your desk.

You pick up your mobile phone and see you have a voicemail from the doctor. You had tried to forget about the tests you had done on Friday, but you have to face up to it.

"This is Stacey from Dr Boucher's rooms, please call back as soon as you can regarding making a follow-up appointment," says the bright receptionist. Your stomach drops as you dial the number to call her back.

They would have told you on the phone if there was nothing, you tell yourself, there must be something on the tests. Dr Boucher has an appointment in twenty minutes and your leave your desk, taking the offer with you, to read in her waiting room.

You have trouble concentrating on the new job specs as you wait for eternity to see the doctor.

"Hi Sophie, thanks for coming in so quickly."

"Of course," you say, your voice catches as your mouth is suddenly as dry as the paper she is shuffling.

"So your tests have come back, and unfortunately, you have tested positive for both chlamydia and gonorrhoea."

"Oh...shit." You can't think of anything else to say, and the doctor waits patiently until you look back to her.

"They're both fairly simply to treat, just a course of antibiotics, but you will need to let any previous partners know."

"Yes," you mumble, clearing your throat. "How far back?"

"That's hard to say, it's likely to be a new infection, but anyone in the last twelve months, to be safe."

You sit, mute, as the doctor explains the treatments and prints out fact sheets and prescriptions.

You can't bear to go back to the office so you buy yourself a coffee around the corner. After about twenty minutes you open up the packet from Candace and read over the job offer. It's a fantastic package, accommodation and travel covered, plus a living away from home bonus on top of the excellent salary. It feels almost too good to refuse.

Somewhere inside you wonder if jumping at this new job is a way to avoid telling Jude. And you'll have to tell James, your ex, he'll gloat you're sure. The irony that he, the serial cheater could have caught something from you, the good one, will definitely amuse him.

Need to see you, come round after work? you text Jude, and you force yourself back to the office.

The rest of the afternoon goes by in a haze and you find yourself answering the door to Jude that night as though no time has passed.

You tell him about the job offer first, to test the waters.

"Whoa, Soph, that's amazing, you have to take it, I mean, don't you?"

You shrug, "I guess. I mean, it's not like I have that much to keep me down here…" you load the silence with all your intention, silently willing Jude to ask you to stay.

He doesn't and the moment stretches out. To fill the silence Jude leans over and kisses you.

"That's not all," you say, turning your face away.

"Really?" He sees your face and his smile fades.

"I had a bit of trouble last week in the…lady area, so I had some tests done."

"Oh."

"Yeah. I have chlamydia. And gonorrhoea. So, umm, probably you do too."

"What the fuck? You gave me the clap? You slut." Jude is unreasonably angry, he stands up and starts to pace your apartment.

"I think I probably got it from you, actually. I'm usually very careful."

"Careful, like we get drunk and you never even ask for a condom? Yeah, real careful. I'm sure you're just as careful with all the guys you randomly fuck."

You can feel tears prickling your eyes. You clench your hands into fists. "I shouldn't have to ask for a condom! You could have offered. You could have insisted. You're as much to blame as me, you were there too." You try to keep your voice under control but you crack and you sit sobbing into your hands.

"Whatever. I don't need this. I'm out." Jude slams the door as he leaves, causing the windows to rattle in their old frames.

"Well, I guess I really don't have anything to keep me here now."

You take the job in Mackay.

The end.

C1.1.5 O2 You chose to go home alone…

"Thanks, but I'm feeling pretty drunk and I reckon best to just go to bed and not be tempted to do anything…uh, ill-advised." You smile at him and sway slightly to emphasise your point.

"I'm pretty drunk too,' he says.

Jude stands there awkwardly for a moment and you impulsively reach up and kiss him. You can feel the alcohol making you clumsy, but he's kissing you back, so it can't be too bad. You make the kiss last as long as you can before slowly pulling away.

"Get home safely, I'll text you when I get home just so you know."

You sit in the cab all the way home thinking about that kiss and enjoying the feel of warm wetness between your thighs it left behind. You would have quite happily slept with Jude that night, but you felt like it was better to take things slowly, especially as he's a work colleague. That being said, there is always that secondment up north if it all goes sideways, you muse as you pay the cabbie and head upstairs.

*

In the morning you feel crusty, your eyes sting when the sunlight touches them and your tongue feels fat and foreign in your mouth. You shuffle through to the kitchen and realise you have nothing to eat. You meant to go shopping yesterday but your preparations for meeting Jude last night got in the way of that.

You decide to go to the café around the corner, there you'll be able to get strong black coffee and something greasy to soak up the hangover. You drag on something from the mostly clean pile of clothing on the floor. It's not your best fashion statement but you're decently covered to be in public at least.

Brett, the hardworking Englishman who owns the café, greets you warmly as you arrive.

"G'mornin love!" His voice seems to boom over the hubbub of the café patrons. "You look a little worse for wear, if I may say."

You smile at him. "Yes, big night, no food at home. I need you to look after me."

"Nothing but the best for you, my girl."

You would have said that Brett was around the same age as you, but whenever he addresses you as 'my girl' it feels paternal.

You follow Brett through the café which is just starting to get busy.

"Last table, just for you,' he says, sitting you in the sunny courtyard at the back of the café. The bright light hurts your eyes, and you hide behind your sunglasses

He takes your order for coffee and bustles back to the front on the shop. The conversation of the other breakfasters is surprisingly soothing and you find yourself drifting off in a sort of meditation.

Halfway through your coffee Brett comes over to your table again. "Sophie, my love, I have this gent here who wants a quiet bite, but there are no more spare tables, you don't mind if he sits with you, do you? No? Good, sit down, Alfred, I'll be with you shortly." Brett doesn't wait for you to answer before showing the man behind you to the empty chair at your table. He's a tall, striking man with dark hair and eyes and a brooding, intense expression.

"Everyone calls me Freddie…except Brett for some reason, and people at work." Freddie extends his hand to you to shake. As he grips your hand his face melts into a smile. What a difference it makes, you think and you leave your hand in his to admire it.

He looks at you expectantly and you drop his hand.

"Sorry, I'm Vera Vague today. Sophie, pleased to meet you."

"What a lovely name. It means wisdom, from the Greek sophos, like philosophy, love of knowledge."

From another man you think it might have sounded pompous or elitist, but you believe he is saying it because he thinks it's interesting, and because he thinks you would like to know.

"I knew it meant wisdom, but didn't realise that was the root. Thanks," you say.

You chat to Freddie a little over breakfast, doing your best to overcome the hangover stupor. It mostly works.

"I'm going to have to head off. I have to get some prep work done for a barbecue at work tomorrow. It was lovely to meet you."

"What do you do for work?"

"I work for the office of the Greens Party in Northcote. You should come by if you're free." His face lights up again in that grin, as he fishes in his wallet. "This is my card, maybe we can do brunch again sometime."

After he's gone you order a takeaway coffee and head home. You realised your fingers are unconsciously stroking Freddie's card in your pocket. After the last night with Jude and the lovely brunch with the somewhat more mysterious Freddie, you think, it never rains but it pours.

*

At work on Monday Candace comes by your desk.

"You know that role we talked about in Mackay? Are you going to apply?"

You had been so caught up in socialising over the weekend you forgot completely about the conversation.

"I haven't really have a chance to think about it. Sorry."

"That's okay. It's a big thing change, and it's not a city like Melbourne. It would be a complete lifestyle change, but I think you would be great at it."

"But what about the new clients down here? How would you go if I left?"

As you talk to Candace you test out the idea of moving in your mind. It's a fantastic opportunity, possibly a career changer, but with the two men on the horizon you don't really want to leave Melbourne, not right now anyway. You remember all the trouble you've had with relationships of the last five years, from Manny, the overly excitable Venezuelan, to Victor who was so reserved you never knew where you stood. If one of these two had potential to be something long-term you'd take that over a job in another state, no matter how good the package.

"Well, there would be a massive hole left behind that we'd have to try to fill, but I think you're the best we have, so sending you on this job would be the best thing for the project." She smiles, "I have mixed feelings about the whole thing."

Fleur Blūm

"If I'm honest, I do too. Career wise it's a fabulous opportunity but life-wise right now... I feel like it would really put a spanner on the works."

You grin to yourself thinking of the possibility that one of these two will turn into something. Then you realise that you haven't sent that message to Freddie, you put it on your mental to do list as soon as you've finished with Candace.

"Oh really?" says Candace, raising a quizzical eyebrow. "Is there goss that I don't know about? Busy weekend?"

You look down at your hands, feeling you face heat with a blush. "Nothing to report yet, but..."

"Playing it close to the chest. I see, very sensible. But I'm dying for some good goss!"

Candace's phone starts ringing in her hand and she looks at it, grimacing. "Gotta take this," she says. She closes the door to her office and you start to understand what a difficult position she's in with the company.

Hi Freddie, this is Sophie. We met yesterday over brunch. Just saying hi, I hope your barbeque went/goes well today. X you text when you sit down at your desk.

You decide to be a little daring putting the kiss at the end; you can always wave it off as a friendly habit if you've misread his interest.

You have an hour or so before you have to head out to client meetings. In that time you think over the Mackay job and decide you'll apply. You can always turn it down when the time comes, if you have a good reason to stay in Melbourne.

When you're waiting downstairs for the tram to head to your meeting on the other side of the city, you see Emily and Calvin slipping off together for lunch. They walk very close together, closer that you would have thought appropriate for just friends. You decide to ask Jude what happened with that email next time you see him.

After work, you meet Felicity at her office building and head out for a Mexican food dinner. With the hectic pace of the weekend you still haven't debriefed each other about the warehouse party and what came afterwards.

"My darling girl, long time no see!" Felicity greets you with a flamboyant hug.

"I know, it's simply been an age since we last had the pleasure of one another's company," you reply, giggling.

Felicity links her arm through yours as you walk towards the Mexican restaurant for cocktails before eating far too many tacos.

"So Jude looked nice," she says, trying to seem less interested than you know she is.

"Yes, I suppose so."

"And? What happened when you left? Did you hook up or what?"

"Nah. I went home on my own. But I met another man on Sunday morning at brunch in the place around the corner, you know the one?"

"With the delicious pommy owner?"

"That's the one. But you, my lovely, you went home with your boy didn't you?" You turn to her and wriggle your eyebrows suggestively.

"Why yes I did. I don't know what I was so anxious about, the boy's crazy for me!"

Over drinks you hear the full story of her night with the Viking, and you tell her all about the relative merits of both men. You see that you still haven't had a reply from Freddie. You're a little disappointed, but he might be busy. You tell yourself not to worry.

You and Felicity call it a night around nine o'clock, you both have to work in the morning. Gone are the days of going out every night and still being able to work the next day.

As you're lying in bed with a trashy horror novel later that evening, you hear your phone chirp.

Hullo! Sorry for the late reply, been totally pummelled with work all day. Looking forward to another catch up, maybe one night this week? We could have a drink or something. X

The first thing you notice is that he's returned your kiss. He must be interested. On the other hand perhaps he sees it as a friendly thing and is merely reciprocating yours.

Even as you make arrangements to meet Freddie you can't seem to shake Jude from your mind. Maybe you could date both of them for a little while, get to know them both a little better before making any commitments. It seems so deliciously decadent.

You arrange to meet with Freddie at a wine bar near the Parliament building in Spring Street on Thursday. It seems like a long time away.

Jude comes over to your desk first thing on Tuesday morning. You're on a call with a client and you wave hello then point to the phone. He stands there expectantly, but you know it's one of your chatty clients.

"Can you just hold on one second?" you say into the phone, before covering it and looking up at Jude. "This is gonna take a while. Should I come round to you when I'm done?"

"No, no, just saying hello. Are you around for lunch?" he asks.

"Uh, yeah, that sounds fine. I'll come by your desk at like, one?"

"I'll meet you out the front."

You nod and get back to the client. As you're talking to the client your mind is drawn back to wondering why Jude wanted to meet out the front. It seems unnecessary, his desk is not that far away and it's almost on your way out anyway.

"I said is that realistic?" your client asks down the phone. You had completely check out of the conversation.

"I'm so sorry, my manager was just trying to catch my attention. What did you ask?"

The client sighs loudly and repeats the question as though he were talking to a child. One of the things you've learnt working with senior executives, in the sales role, that you never knew working for Max in analysis, is that older men can be real arseholes when they want to be.

The call lasts another twenty minutes, twenty minutes in which you try very hard not to get distracted by thoughts of Jude and Freddie.

You barely have time to run to the bathroom before you have to meet Jude downstairs.

"You know the applications for the Mackay job are due on Friday, right?" Candace calls as you rush past her office.

"I know, I'm onto it!" you call back.

Downstairs Jude is leaning against one of the marble pillars looking tense. He's framed in sunlight and you feel a warm wash of arousal as you approach.

116

"I thought you were standing me up," he says, pushing away from the wall and starting up the street.

"I'm only two minutes late, I was still on the phone to that client!"

"Huh, well, some people are just insensitive to the effect they have on other people," he says.

You feel like the comment is addressed more to you than to the client.

"Anyway, where are we headed?" You ignore his tone and change the subject.

"I thought we might try this coffee place I've heard about. They're just about the best thing in this section of town. Everyone I know has been and I haven't managed to try it yet."

"Sounds good."

Jude walks quickly, and doesn't seem to be much interested in conversation. When he abruptly turns into a tiny, hole in the wall café, you see what he means, it's full of the trendiest people. The minute interior is decorated with exposed light bulbs hanging over the counters, a huge graffiti mural, dark wood tables and mismatched chairs.

"Gosh, it's busy in here!" you say.

"That's how you know it's good," he says, raising his voice over the hubbub.

You both order takeaway coffees and baguettes and stand in the street as the coffees are made. After taking a couple of bites of his baguette Jude leans over to you.

"Sorry I was a bit snappy, I get kind of angry when I'm hungry?" He smiles at you and you remember what it felt like to kiss those lips. Warmth starts to spread in your groin.

"I get like that sometimes too."

"So, Saturday night was fun…" he says, leaving the comment unfinished in the air.

"Two lattes?" a bearded barista yells out of the serving window.

"That's us," you say, avoiding Jude's last reference and rushing to take the coffees.

You hand him his latte and he starts to amble away towards a small open square with benches.

"You didn't answer the question," he says sitting next to you. He sits so close that his thigh is pressed against yours.

"What question is that?" you ask.

"I wanted to know whether you enjoyed that kiss on Saturday night. I hope you didn't have so much to drink that you forgot." He winks, smiling in that way he has, as though he might eat you right there.

"I remember. I have been thinking about it a lot, actually." You take a sip of your coffee and let out and involuntary sigh. "Mmm. That is good!"

Jude takes a sip from his latte and nods.

"I guess I'm just wondering how sensible it is to, uh, date a co-worker," you say.

"There are a lot of potential areas for awkwardness, but on the plus side, we don't work in the same team, and we really don't have much that to do with each other so what is there to lose?" he asks.

"It's against company policy," you say, hoping Jude will have an argument for that too.

"That's true, but one, they really can't enforce a non-fraternisation clause, it's not the army and what I do outside of work time is none of the company's business. Unless I suppose it could reasonably be shown to affect the company's reputation, which this wouldn't. And two, who would need to know? That's part of why I wanted to meet you out the front instead of having you come pick me up at my desk. Plausible deniability." He takes a huge bite from his baguette without moving his eyes off you.

"You've certainly given it a lot of thought..." you say.

What's the harm? You think, it's too early to say there is anything exclusive going on between you and Freddie and Jude is an attractive, employed, hardworking guy.

"I suppose there's no reason anyone would need to know," you add, staring at him over your coffee cup as you take another gorgeous sip.

"What I'd really like to do is kiss you again right here, but it's too exposed and I'm sure someone from work would go blabbing, so, how about I make you dinner tomorrow? It's very quiet and private at my house, I live on my own. No possibility of being busted by a colleague."

You think about it for a moment before agreeing. As long as I don't stay over, it's a work night and that it would be too soon anyway, you promise yourself.

You get back to your desk and see that you have a text message from Freddie.

Looking forward to drinks. I really enjoyed out chat last weekend and I'm ready for a night off from working. xx

Now there's two kisses, you think with a smile.

I'll take your mind off work, I promise, you reply, adding a winky face.

Is it okay to have dinner with boy from work tomorrow and drinks with boy from café Thurs? you text

119

Felicity. You want her to tell you it's okay to see them both.

Totally! Lunch Friday to debrief? she writes back immediately. She must be having a slow day at work to reply so quickly.

Yes. For sure!

*

On Wednesday night you head home from work early so that you can get yourself ready for dinner with Jude. He lives on the other side of the city from you in St Kilda so you decide to drive there. You have a quick shower and select and outfit which is more casual than anything you would wear to work; skinny jeans and a T-shirt with a nice cardigan over the top. You do a final check of your makeup and head out the door with plenty of time to get through the evening traffic.

Jude opens the door wearing the suit he was in at work with an apron over the top. His apron and hands are covered in flour and he waves you in without giving you a hug.

"What're you making?" you ask as you follow him through to the kitchen.

Jude's apartment is small but very modern, with massive blank white walls and beige furniture. It's quite minimalist and you're not sure you like it. It feels cold in the apartment although the temperature hasn't dropped.

"I decided to make you gnocchi. I really love making it from scratch but never bother to do it when it's just me." He grins at you and goes back to cutting little dumplings from a long sausage of gnocchi-to-be.

"I brought some red wine," you say, brandishing the bottle that you pulled from the cupboard at the last minute. "Sorry, I didn't think to ask if you liked red."

"Just pop it on the table," he says, without looking at it.

Jude made a simple tomato-based sauce to go with the gnocchi and it's delicious. You eat far too much of it, and between you drink the whole bottle of wine.

Jude clears the table and comes back with another bottle of wine. He sits down next to you and puts his hand on your shoulder.

"So, shall we open this one?" His eyes are sparkling and mischievous.

"Why not!" you say, warm and happily full of wine and pasta.

He puts the bottle on the table and moves his hand to your thigh. He leans in to kiss you and you feel the wall between you disappear. You're suddenly clawing at his shirt trying to get it off him, the fuzzy feeling of the wine has moved to create a hot spot your groin. All you can think of is the need to feel his skin against yours.

"Mmm, yes, yes," you mumble into his hair as he pulls up your T-shirt and buries his face between your breasts.

"Come with me," he says, standing up and pulling you with him into the bedroom. He has candles sitting around the room, casting a flickering yellow-orange light over the bed, which is also beige.

Jude throws you onto the bed playfully and pulls your cardigan and T-shirt off over your head in one movement. He's unbuttoning his shirt as you unbuckle his belt and trousers.

Jude's torso is beautiful, sculpted from time spent at the gym and covered in a light layer of brown hair. You run your fingers upwards over it towards his erect nipples.

He brings his mouth down to yours, removing his pants and underwear as he does. He is now naked and hard in front of you. Your hands move towards his cock, but he gently bats you away.

"Greedy girl," he says.

You pretend innocence, "I'm not allowed?"

"Not yet." He pushes you back so you're lying on the bed as he undoes your jeans and peels them away. He climbs on top of you, straddling you, his erection bouncing as he does.

He takes your hand and moves it to himself, sighing as you stroke him. His hips twitch and he moves a little further up the bed. You raise up your head and tease him with your tongue.

Jude reaches down, running his fingers through your hair, encouraging you to take more of his cock into your mouth. You oblige pushing yourself all the way down.

In this position, your neck is bent at an uncomfortable angle, and while you want to continue you need to change position.

You push his hips away and he looks down at you confused.

"Stand up," you say, attempting a seductive tone.

You wriggle off the bed and kneel in front of him. You reach your hands around and grab his buttocks, firm, gym-trained cheeks. You slide him in your mouth again and use your hands to push his pelvis towards you.

Jude groans in pleasure, tangling his fingers in your hair.

"You're very good at this. Mmm," he says, his voice a little ragged in his excitement.

"Put a finger in my arse," he says suddenly. You look up at him briefly, before bringing your middle finger to your mouth and coating it in saliva.

You gently push your way into his arse, his cock back in your mouth. Almost instantly he orgasms violently, squirting hot cum down your throat. You're caught by surprise and try not to choke.

After a moment he stops twitching and you pull away. He sways a little before stumbling over to the bed, falling onto it.

You look around for the bathroom and quickly wash your hands. You use your cupped hand to drink some water from the tap.

Before joining Jude on the bed you grab the second bottle of wine from the table. You put the wine on one of the bedside tables and snuggle yourself up behind Jude.

"That was fun," you say, stroking along his shoulder and arm. You can feels the dampness in your underwear left by your own excitement and you are trying to get him interested in some more fooling around.

"Mmm, definitely," he says sounding sleepy.

"You want some more wine?"

"Huh? Uh, no, we've got work tomorrow. It's probably time I went to bed, actually."

"Oh right," you say, disappointed.

"I'm going to shower. You should probably get going, you can't wear that to work," he points to the pile of your clothes on the floor. "And we can't turn up together either."

"Yeah. Right," you say. You are starting to feel very drunk and rejected.

"Can I leave my car in your street?" You don't really want to drive home right now.

"Uh, well you can, but you'll probably get a fine, they're total arseholes." Jude gets up and collects your jeans and top, holding them out to you.

"Thanks." It's very tempting to snatch your clothes from his hands but you manage not to.

Jude heads into the bathroom and turns on the water in the shower.

CHOOSE:

If you call a taxi and come back for your car later go to p 125

If you decide to drive home, go to p 140.

C1.1.6 O1 You chose to call a taxi and come back for your car later…

You rush out of Jude's apartment, holding back tears. You had convinced yourself this was going to be something good but Jude is just interested in his own pleasure.

As you wobble down towards your car you know you're way too drunk to drive home. You decide to risk the parking fine, which you probably deserve for having such poor taste in men, and come back for the car tomorrow.

Out on the main road you wave down a taxi and head home.

"You alright, love?" the driver asks as you step out.

"Yes, thank you. I just didn't have a very good day."

"Hope tomorrow's better," he says and he pulls away from the kerb.

You stand under the water of the shower for the second time today and you let the drunken tears flow. *This is why I don't date co-workers,* you think.

Thursday at work is tough. Your head hurts from the wine and your eyes are puffy from crying. You consider cancelling on Freddie but you worry that would put him off.

Hey, you wanna get food instead of a drink? I need a night off alcohol, you text him as you return from lunch.

Oh dear. Tell me about it later. Meet you at the same spot and we'll find somewhere around with food.

Sophie's Path

You're meeting him in Spring Street, but you hope he's interested in having something in Chinatown. That's what you feel like; a big brothy soup from one of the myriad little restaurants in Little Bourke Street.

Freddie leans in to kiss you on the cheek when you meet.

"Big night last night?" he asks.

"I had a small accident which resulted in the unexplained disappearance of quite a lot of red wine. I'm feeling it," you reply, with a weary smile.

"You could have postponed our date," he says, your heart gives a little flutter at the word date.

"No, no, I wanted to see you. I'm sorry if I'm bad company. I hope I can hold it together long enough for some dinner. I'll make it up to you on the weekend."

Freddie smiles and it always takes you by surprise how much lighter he seems when he does.

"Shall we find something to eat then?" he asks, turning to offer you his elbow.

You slip your hand through it and he clamps you tightly against his side. You can feel his heart beating through his jacket. It might be your imagination, but it seems to be thumping quite hard. You smile to yourself as Freddie leads you down a series of small alleys to a hidden treasure of a restaurant.

You eat and chat and you would be having an excellent night but your body is screaming to go home to bed.

"I think we should probably call it a night," Freddie says as the waiter takes away the plates that used to be filled with delicious dumplings.

"I'm okay," you say.

"You don't look okay. You look green. Shall we share a taxi home? You're just around the corner from me."

You look at him; it's very sweet for him to offer.

"That would be lovely. Thank you."

The taxi driver takes the corners too fast and overuses the horn, but the two of you arrive back at your house uninjured.

"I'll bid you goodnight here and walk to mine," Freddie says at your gate.

"Thank you for understanding. I'm never drinking on a week night again. I promise."

"Don't promise that," Freddie says with a wink. "Have a good sleep. I'll talk to you soon."

He leans in to kiss you on the lips. He's gentle and keeps his mouth firmly closed. The kiss only lasts a second but you want it to last forever.

"Be safe, see you soon," you say after he pulls away.

You watch him walk down the street then turn to head inside. Your eyes are heavy and gritty with tiredness. You strip off your clothes and fall into bed. You're asleep before you've even had time to think about how comfortable it is.

When you wake up your pillow is covered in smears of makeup and you feel like you have a small furry animal living in your mouth, but at least your headache is gone.

You meet Felicity for lunch at the Japanese place you both like and order beef and noodles. You still feel overtired and a little uncoordinated after two nights out in a row, and noodles with chopsticks were probably a bad idea. If you have to ask for a fork you'll just have to swallow your pride and deal with the pitying looks of the staff.

Felicity sits across from you with a sashimi pack, smothering everything in wasabi and soy.

"So, you haven't told me about your dates!" she says just before shoving an entire piece of sashimi into her mouth.

"Well, Jude is a definite no."

"Oh?" Felicity mumbles.

"He got me really drunk–well, I got myself really drunk when he made dinner–and then we fooled around– no, actually he got me to suck him off–and then when he was done he kicked me out and jumped in the shower. He's sent me a follow up text like 'When are you free to come visit me again' but I haven't replied" you break off. "Oh shit! My car is still out the front of his place in St Kilda."

"Why did you leave your car at his place?" Felicity asks.

"I was too drunk to drive home. Jude could have offered me his couch if he didn't want to share the bed, but no, he just turfed me out."

"Right, Jude's a no then?"

"He's a dick. And I think he's a bit of a player; doesn't seem to be particularly interested in having a proper relationship. Like he wants a colleague with benefits whenever it suits him."

Now that you say it aloud you realise that this is the reason you felt so uncomfortable about the idea of dating a co-worker. Not so much because of the potential for awkwardness, but because you were worried you were a conquest, not a person.

"Gross. Moving on."

"So last night I went out for dinner with Freddie. He was very understanding of my wanting to avoid alcohol. I mean, obviously I didn't tell him it was coz I drank a whole bottle of wine with another dude, but–anyway, he shared a taxi home with me and we had a little peck on the mouth but nothing super exciting."

"Have you heard since last night?" she asks around a mouthful.

"Umm," you check your phone briefly, "no, nothing so far, but he's usually busy during the day. He hardly ever texts unless it's super early, or super late."

"What does he do?"

"He's some sort of advisor to a member of the Greens, I think. He did tell me but it went in one ear and out the other." You catch yourself smiling foolishly and you go back to trying to fit your noodles into your mouth.

"Send him something now," Felicity says.

"No, I'll wait till later."

"Do it now. Invite him to have dinner with you. Somewhere local, so you can go back to yours if it goes well. Do it!" She points her chopsticks at you.

You laugh. "Alright, jeez."

"Hi Freddie. Thanks for last night. Are you free for dinner tomorrow? I promise not to be green around the gills this time."

You show the message to Felicity, who nods her approval, and send it off.

"So, Eric is…fucking hot, oh my God," Felicity blurts. "I've been saving that up until after you'd told me your boy news but, wow. Just, wow."

You grin at her and feed most of your noodles into your mouth clumsily while she tells you, in graphic detail, about the tall blond Viking-type she hooked up with at the party. It seems like much more than a week ago.

You check your phone to see if Freddie has replied, but he hasn't.

"Ah, crap, I have to run," you say as Felicity starts to tell you about the thing Eric does with his tongue that creates a visual in your mind you're not sure you'll ever be able to forget.

"Oh." Felicity makes a pouty face. "Alright, fine. I guess I have to get back to work too. Don't work too hard, it's Friday afternoon and you've had a big week." She stands up to hug you before striding towards the door.

When you get back there's a note from Candace on your desk.

Application for the QLD job! it says.

You had been avoiding doing the application all week, partly being distracted by men. But it's partly because you're feeling anxious about such a big step up after having only been in the sales team for a few months.

Picking up the note, you walk over to Candace's office.

"Got a minute?" you ask.

"'Course," she says, waving you in.

"I got your note." You hold it up, "I'm really in two minds about it."

"Pull up a pew and let's talk."

"I know in my head that the opportunity is really good and that I'd earn heaps and get a great addition to my resume, but I just don't feel confident. I'm also not sure I want to live in far north Queensland."

"I know what you mean. I've had plenty of applications from the slacker types who seem to think it's a paid holiday but hardly any from people who I think will actually do the job." She shakes her head.

"Oh," you say. You feel a tug of guilt about your procrastination. The project might fail if Candace doesn't get a good applicant, but you can't justify doing something that might completely screw up your chances with Freddie.

"When does Aubrey want the secondment to start again?" you ask.

"ASAP really. June at the latest."

"Right." You heave a sigh and stand up.

"You have to do what's right for you, of course, but just think about it, will you, Soph? Please?" Candace says.

"I'll give it some more thought."

You head back to your desk and start updating your resume and application. You check your phone for replies from Freddie every few minutes but by 4:30 p.m. there's still nothing.

Applications are due by the end of the day and you tell yourself that you can't live your life waiting for boys to text you back. You send the application to Candace as you head out the door for the weekend.

"Thank you! Thank you!" Candace says as you go past, the relief in her voice making it wobble a little.

"No worries. Have a good weekend."

You catch the tram down to St Kilda to collect your car, the Friday night crowds are awful and you have to stand all the way with your face right in the armpit of a very tall, very rotund man.

Sophie's Path

Your car is exactly where you left it, outside the apartment building where Jude lives. You give a small shiver as you approach, hoping he isn't on his way home and you won't have to speak to him. You'll have to see him around the office at some point and explain you're not interested in pursuing anything but you secretly hope he'll just take the hint if you don't reply.

There are no tickets on your windscreen, and you breathe easier when you start the car and drive off into the evening traffic without seeing Jude. You phone jangles the text message alert from inside your handbag as you drive down the hill in Punt Road. You ignore it until you get home.

Hey! Thanks for last night. Dinner tomorrow sounds awesome. You can come to mine if you like. I'm feeling pretty burned out after a super busy week so pizza and a movie is about the most I can do. xx

You're hesitant to go to Freddie's place, mostly because you don't want a repeat of the humiliation of Wednesday. Freddie isn't like that, you think, he's much more of a gentleman.

Okay. Sounds ideal, you text back.

You park in your designated parking bay, next to your storage area under the block of apartments where you live and climb up the back stairs to your floor. Now that home is in sight the weight of the week hits you hard.

You find a can of soup in the cupboard for dinner and fall asleep watching a trashy rom-com from your collection.

Freddie's place isn't far from yours; it only takes you five minutes to walk there on Saturday night. It occurs to you that he's probably been within reach for the entire two years you've been living here but your paths never crossed.

He greets you with a smile and another brief kiss on the lips.

"Thanks for coming over. I'm sorry I can't be more energetic but I'm a bit of a home body really. Better you know that sooner rather than later, right?"

You giggle. "I like to pretend I'm a party person, but a night in on the couch with a movie and good company is pretty great."

He takes your hand and leads you down the hallway of his brick terrace house.

"My housemate is out at the moment, but may or may not come back later on," he says as you enter into the small but cosy lounge room. The décor is a little bit confused, a woven rag rug, like you get from those hippie places, covers the grey carpet and two sofas face the T.V. One of the couches is covered in a sort of red-brown woollen fabric, and looks like it might have been scrounged from hard rubbish, and the other is a cream brocade three seater. You guess the cream one belongs to Freddie and the other to his housemate. You can't imagine anyone owning both couches.

"That one's Jessie's," he says, indicating the red-brown couch.

You laugh. "You read my mind. I was trying to figure out how two such, uh, uniquely different couches came to live here."

"Everyone thinks that. I've known Jessie for a long time, I love her, she's what you might call an arty type. I like to keep her around because she stops me getting too far up my own arse."

"You have to have people around you to keep your feet on the ground," you say.

You hover at near the doorway of the lounge room, not sure where you should sit. If you go for the cream couch, where Freddie is bound to sit it might indicate too much interest too soon, or the red-brown one, which might give off an overly cold impression.

Freddie looks up and sees you frowning. He takes your hand.

"Come sit here," he says, leading you to the cream couch bringing you with him.

"This is the pizza place, it's not the world fanciest date night dinner, but I figure we have time to get fancy later," he says and hands you the menu.

"I don't think I've ever had a pizza from these guys before. I'm looking forward to it."

After phoning through an order for a whole pizza each, allowing for leftovers, he says, Freddie puts his phone on the coffee table. He does it very carefully and his eyes linger on it in a strange way. You wonder if he's working himself up to something with a flutter in your stomach.

He looks up at you, his intense soulful eyes seem to look straight into your soul, he takes a deep breath. "So what do you want to watch?" he asks.

"That's not what you were going to say." You stare back at him, aware that you're both extremely sober but still wanting to take hold of the moment.

"It's not," he replies. "I was going to kiss you, but uh, I chickened out."

"I see," you say, reaching out and placing your hand on his thigh. He twitches involuntarily and you almost pull your hand away.

"Sorry, I'm a bit…anxious." He puts his hand on top of yours on his thigh.

"We don't have to do anything, y' know, pizza and a movie can be just that." *Even though I really want more,* you think.

"I know." His fingers wander across yours though he seems unaware of moving them.

You lean over and kiss him gently. He's stiff at first but melts a little at a time until he is kissing you back. His hands are up around your jaw and in your hair, and he has moved up and over you so that you're lying beneath his lean body.

You sink into the couch and gently try to wriggle yourself into a more comfortable position. You run your hands over Freddie's shoulders and back, enjoying the warm friction created by his checked flannel shirt. You are careful to keep your hands outside his clothes; his hands are still cupping your face and neck.

You can feel his erection beneath your leg, the heat of his groin meeting yours through your jeans. You desperately want to reach under his shirt to touch his skin but you also know that this moment can only happen once. The newness of his lips, the tantalising unknown of his skin, the urgency and the torturous bliss of delaying the gratification.

Freddie and you kiss on the couch, heedless of time passing, until you're interrupted by the buzzing of the doorbell.

He pulls away, looking somewhat dazed.

"Can you get the door?" he says, looking at his obviously engorged groin.

You laugh. "Sure." You smile and straighten your clothing before trotting back down the hallway to the front door.

As you reach the door you realise you have no money with you, but the delivery driver doesn't ask for any. Freddie would have paid with his card when he ordered, you think. Your mind is still on his lips and the smell of his skin. You can feel your own arousal soaking your underpants as you sit yourself back down on the cream sofa.

Freddie has rearranged himself so that his hard-on is not as obvious and seems to be intent on eating rather than going straight back to making out. You ignore the little twinge of disappointment.

"I thought we could watch something old school. I have 'Never Ending Story', 'Dark Crystal', 'Labyrinth', and a few others. I find I never get sick of watching them."

The two of you flip open your pizza boxes and the sudden aroma of pizza reminds you that you haven't eaten for several hours.

You grab a slice of pizza before answering, "I am happy to watch whatever you want. It's your house, so you pick."

You take a huge bite out of the slice of pizza as he ponders the decision.

"Alright. 'The Dark Crystal'."

You each eat almost an entire pizza each and wash them down with cold soft drinks from Freddie's fridge. You're filled with nostalgic glee rewatching the film, and Freddie wraps his arm around you.

When the credits roll you feel sleepy and safe and you never want to leave. Except your bladder is full of soft drink and you can't hold it any longer.

"Bathroom?" you say, reluctantly peeling yourself out of the cocoon.

"Back through the kitchen." Freddie waves his hand in the direction of a plain pine door leading off from the kitchen.

When you get back, Freddie has put the remaining pizza into the fridge and cleaned up. He's leaning on the kitchen bench.

He sweeps you into his arms as you go past, planting his mouth firmly on yours. The urgency that you denied earlier on the couch has returned more strongly and his hands are all over your body. You press him to you and slip your hands up the back of his shirt, running your fingers along his skin.

Just as Freddie manages to unclip your bra you hear a key turning in the front door.

"Ssh, that's Jessie. Be cool." He pulls away from you, his cheeks flushed and his pants askew. He leans against the bench, hiding his arousal.

Jessie breezes in and goes straight into her room without coming as far as the kitchen.

"Quick, my bedroom, before she comes back out." Freddie grabs your hand and you race down the hallway, thundering towards his bedroom.

You are both giggling and breathless when he slams the door shut behind him and pushes you backwards to the bed.

"Ssh! Ssh!" he whispers.

"Sorry," you reply, doing your best to calm your laughter.

Sophie's Path

Instead of waiting for you stop Freddie covers your mouth with his and unbuttons his shirt. Once he has thrown it to the floor you see that his upper arms and chest are covered in tattoos. You make a mental note to ask about those later.

After the whole evening of build-up and in spite of Freddie's repeated protestations of being tired, you have wild, passionate, athletic sex.

As you lie next to him, a thin sheen of sweat glistening on both of you, you decide that you're not going to Queensland. You want to give this, whatever it is, with Freddie a chance and leaving for a secondment, no matter how good the money, is not what's going to make you happy.

You rest your head in Freddie's shoulder and listen to his breathing.

You got the guy! You didn't get the promotion, but you didn't even want it.

C 1.1.6 O2 You chose to drive home…

You get dressed and splash some water from the kitchen sink onto your face, blotting it with paper towel. Your makeup is all over the place and you feel strongly like you might cry.

"I'm heading off then," you call to Jude over the running water.

"Okay, bye then."

You're miserable as you make your way to your car. Your belly feels gross, stodgy and hard with all that pasta, wine, and cum mixed with your mood create horrible nausea.

You get in the car and you know it's a bad idea, but all you can think about is getting home; back to your own bed.

As you drive up Punt Road back towards the northern side of Melbourne you feel your eyelids drooping. You wind down the window to allow the cold breeze to wash over your face but it doesn't help. As you roll down the big hill towards the Yarra you close your eyes just briefly. In that moment you don't realise that the lights are red and you roll through the intersection at full speed and slam into the corner of the bridge.

You have killed yourself driving home drunk.
At least you didn't take anyone else with you.
You lose.

C1.1.1 O2 You chose to go back to your desk…

"Well, I better get back to it, or these will get cold before I get them to the boss," you say, picking up the two coffees.

Jude laughs quietly. "Yeah, see you around." He makes no move to push away from the bench he's leaning on and continues to stare off into middle distance.

When you poke your head around Candace's door she's off the phone and the shadows under her eyes seem darker. She looks up as you come in and she sees the coffee her face brightens a little.

"What would I do without you, Sophie." She sips the coffee and sighs heavily.

"Anything else I can do?" you ask, hovering next to her desk.

"Sit down. I may as well tell you about it now." Her voice matches her tired face.

"Tell me about what?"

She takes another sip of her coffee. "Aubrey has just been on the phone. He was telling me how well you did in the meeting this morning. He's at one of the offices of a property developer client, anyway he was telling me that they're looking at opening an office in Mackay, you know, in northern Queensland, and they asked Aubrey if they could take someone from the company to help get things rolling up there."

"That sounds exciting," you say, suddenly worried that Aubrey wants to steal your boss away and put you in her place. You'd love to do Candace's job one day, but you thought you'd have another two years of training.

"He wants me to make a recommendation from my team to the post. He wants a candidate by Friday next week. With all the other shit I'm dealing with at the moment I don't know how I'm going to deal with being one person down by the end of the month. And that's before spending all my time wading through a bunch of applicants to get a replacement who won't get effective for at least three months…" she trails off and looks at the phone handset.

"I'm sorry I shouldn't be burdening you with this, it's not your job. I'll work it out, but y' know, you're here so I'm afraid you copped it," she says.

"That's totally fine," you reply. Candace obviously needs reassurance but you're not sure what you can possibly say.

"I'll put it to everyone, and then you'll all have a chance to put in an application, that's probably fair. I'll recommend my choice to Aubrey next week. Is it something you'd consider, a secondment up north?"

"Uhh…" you struggle to put your thoughts in order. "It's honestly not something I've ever thought about."

"You should think about it, Sophie, I could never replace you, of course, but I think you'd do a good job up there."

"Yes, it would be a great opportunity," you say, your mind blank. "I'm going to get back to it. I've still got to get up to speed for this meeting tomorrow morning."

As you walk back to your desk you decide that you'd better talk it over with Felicity when you meet next.

Drink after work? you text her when you sit back down.

Yeah, cool, meet you downstairs? Usually she would be chattier in texts especially given that you blew her off earlier, you think she must be distracted.

You meet her in the bar at the bottom of her building at close to 6 p.m. It's a strange space, tucked into a corner opposite the shiny steel lifts. The bar is dark wood, and the carpets seem to be dark green, Felicity is already there, standing next to a high black table with a cocktail in front of her.

"Sorry I'm late," you say giving her a long hug.

"You work too hard, skip out on lunch and then leave me hanging in the same day."

"I know, I know. Candace offered me a job in Queensland. Okay, she didn't technically offer the job to me; she said that I should apply for the secondment and that I was her preferred candidate so I am sort of assuming she wants to offer it to me-"

"What sort of job is it?" Felicity cuts in.

You explain the job as leaving out the spin that Candace put on it though, just laying down the facts.

"Wow, that is pretty big," Felicity says when you finish.

"I don't want to go, but part of me thinks that's just fear, you know? Like do I just wanna stick in my comfort zone. I mean think of how it would look for my career? I've basically been handpicked for this job. I just don't know how to feel."

"It's a big decision, babe. You have to be true to yourself whatever you decide."

The two of you stand quietly for a while.

"These really aren't very good are they?" you say, putting your empty cocktail glass back on the high table.

Felicity laughs. "No, they aren't, but if you were on time we could have avoided buying a drink from here!" She pokes her tongue out at you playfully.

"Wanna come round for pizza then?"

"No, I'm having dinner with Eric at seven-thirty." She hesitates. "I mean unless you need me?"

"No, of course not. I just wanted to make up for lunch. I'm excited to hear about how the dinner went later though!"

You give her a short hug, squeezing her small frame to you briefly, and both walk out into busy King Street. You watch as people, mostly in suits, wander past. It's well after rush hour there are still plenty of pedestrians and taxis.

The evening is now open in front of you. On a normal Wednesday night you would head home, have some dinner, or maybe do a yoga class, but you feel restless. You're jealous of Felicity. She didn't call it a date, but you know that she wants it to be.

It's hard not to be a little bit resentful of her, it seems like she's constantly got new men on the horizon while you're still trying to recover from the catastrophe which was your last relationship.

James Byron. Charming, spontaneous and fun to be around. He's fantastic for a good time, he knows all the ways to get you drunk, or high, or doing things you wouldn't normally do. On the other hand, he's manipulative, impulsive, and cannot be serious.

But damn, he's gorgeous. When he's there looking at you, he makes you feel beautiful, desirable; like the only woman in the world.

You haven't spoken to him since the breakup, but you're feeling lonely, and a little more than tipsy. You take out your phone and call him.

"Hello, stranger," he says when he answers.

"Hi." Now that you hear his voice you wonder what you're doing.

"I've been thinking about you a lot recently. About the times we had, I wanted to call you but I know you said I had to stay away. Look at me respecting your boundaries!" he says.

You can't help but laugh. He's as charming as ever and you don't even try to resist him.

"Thank you, babe," you say. It slips out before you can stop it. Babe.

"What are you doing now?" he asks. This is exactly why you called him, so he would ask you this question. You know him well enough to know that anything he frequently throws off a social engagement for a better offer.

"I'm just in the city, I had a drink with Felicity, but she's off for a date. What are you doing."

He laughs, it's a deep rumble almost like a purr and you feel your insides start to vibrate in response.

"Ah, I see." You can almost hear the eyebrow he's raising down the phone. "I'm just at Madame Brussels, in Bourke St, with some of the guys, come up and call me when you're here. I'll ditch them and we can...hang out."

You know this is a bad idea. You and James cannot be friends with benefits, part of you is still in love with him but your skin is screaming out to be touched.

"I'm going to get in a taxi now, and I'll pick you up. Be outside in ten." You hear your own voice take on a tone of command you haven't heard for a long time.

"Yes, ma'am," James says, his throaty purr rings in your ears after he's hung up.

As promised, he's standing on the street as your taxi pulls up, he's draped his suit jacket over his arm and is wearing a vest and shirt. James is immaculately dressed as always, his hair is slightly longer than it used to be, the golden-brown strands spilling over his collar and even from the taxi you see his strong jaw, and proud nose. He jumps into the back seat as soon as you pull up.

"Hi," he says.

You give the taxi driver the address of your apartment before leaning over to James and kissing him hard on the mouth. Instantly your senses are full of him. He's wearing the same cologne, a smell that will always arouse you, even on other men who happen to walk by wearing it, your body seems to respond primally.

He tastes of whiskey, and given the flush in his cheeks he's had a few, probably nothing to eat either. As you kiss him you remember his betrayal, but that's not something for you to think about now.

You barely speak as he follows you up to your apartment. You grip his hand and he seems to sense that this is not an occasion for talking.

Once inside the door you rip each other's clothes off. His own scent is mixed with his cologne, and you bury your face in his densely-haired chest, breathing in the hot, familiar smell.

You frantically grasp at one another, desperate to be closer. You want him to be a part of your body, you want him to crawl inside you and stay there. Instead you take him to your bedroom and get as close to engulfing him as possible.

Sweat shines on your bodies. You wrap him in your legs and arms as he lies on top of you, sliding himself in and out of your body. You want more of him, to fully possess him.

When you finally finish, panting and spent, you have no idea how long you've been together, the idea of time slipped away.

James curls behind you, and you pull his arms around you. You don't want to break the spell; the cocoon of physical connection that you've made.

If you talk you'll remember why you had to leave him, but right now, in this silent moment you can forget all of that.

You fall asleep locked together, but when you wake up sometime later you realise that you're alone again. It's light outside but it feels very early. You check the clock and it's 6:30 a.m.

You walk out into your living room to look for James still naked, but you know he's not there. He never wanted to do the morning after thing even then you lived together.

The desolation you feel at finding yourself alone again, after the illusion that you created with him last night of being a single entity, intertwined with him, is so much heavier than the loneliness you felt last night.

You step into the shower and wash the traces of his smell from your skin. As the water washes over your face you let your tears flow freely, disappearing into the water. You know that you can't bear to go to work today, it's just too hard to put on your professional face and meet with clients and tell them how great they are.

Fleur Blüm

You pull the sheets off your bed, getting a strong waft of James and the things you did together. Every reminder of him is like a fresh cut. You didn't know that you could feel this raw, but you know it's your own fault. You allowed a beautiful, charming snake into your bed again, and it did what it was designed to do; inject you with its venom and slither away.

You take the job in Mackay, hoping that six months away from James will cure you of him, but when then you realise you're pregnant. You're forever tied to a man who will always hurt you. You lose.

C1 O2 You chose to ignore them and go out to lunch…

Your belly grumbles loudly as you head back to your desk. Knowing that there is nothing but a can of supermarket soup in there, you decide to have lunch with your bestie.

Meet you at the sandwich place in ten?"

Felicity replies almost immediately. Affirmative!

"Are you coming to the party on Saturday night?" Felicity says as soon as she sees you. She's been going on about the dockside rave for two weeks.

"Really? No hi, how are you?" you reply as you pull up a stool. The furnishings in the little shop are low wooden stools and low tables packed tightly together. It makes it very awkward to eat there, maybe it's to discourage lingering, you think to yourself.

"I know how you are, you're frazzled because it's Wednesday and you had the staff meeting, and you're frustrated because the Candy Queen ran off and left you in the lurch with the Big Boss and you don't want to talk about work." She grins at you. "Tell me I'm wrong."

You make muttering noises under your breath, and then look up at her. "You've never admitted to being wrong in your whole life. And yes I am still coming to the thing. Stop asking, I've said yes the last hundred times you've checked, haven't I?"

"I know but it's not your scene and I keep thinking you'll find an excuse. And if you don't come, I will actually die."

"You won't die. But you may have to talk to that boy you like on your own, which I suppose is about the same," you say.

Felicity sticks her tongue out at ycu. "So food?"

You look longingly at the cabinet filled with sandwiches and wraps. "Definitely," you say.

*

For the rest of the week you are busy with the new client Candace has pulled from a colleague and given to you. The reasons she gave you: you're the more senior employee and the client is difficult. After a week of chasing your own tail, you're starting to resent the amount of work she is giving you.

On Saturday evening you're equal parts excited and nervous about this party. You bought yourself a new outfit last weekend, and it seemed perfect in the shop, but standing in front of the mirror at home all you can see is the lumps and imperfections that you think the tight dress highlights. Not to mention the loud floral pattern on it. The shop assistant insisted it was 'very you', but it doesn't feel like it now.

"It's a cocktail party, you will be surrounded ridiculous outfits, it will be fine," you tell your reflection sternly, she doesn't seem impressed but you're already running late and changing your dress won't help.

You finish off the glass of white wine and make one final adjustment to your hair before grabbing your jacket and tiny clutch bag and rushing out the door. As you come around the corner at the end of your street you can see the tram approaching.

CHOOSE:

If you decide to run for the tram, go to <u>p 151</u>

If you decide to walk and get the next one, go to <u>p 194</u>.

C1.2 O1 You chose to run to catch the tram…

You decide to run for the tram. In the giant, ridiculous, gorgeous high-heeled shoes you're wearing you immediately regret it, but once you've started you may as well run the rest of the short distance to the stop. You arrive with ten seconds to spare, which you use to tuck a stray strand of hair back into place and wriggle the skirt of your dress back down your thighs. The balls of your feet are throbbing after the run, and you hope they settle down by the time you get into the city.

There are plenty of seats and you head towards the back where you can have four seats all to yourself. Interactions with strangers on trams are best avoided in your experience. Most people seem to put as much space as is available between themselves and another passenger.

Your going out handbag is small, covered in black sequins and has a silver chain shoulder strap. It barely has room for your phone, wallet and keys, so you don't have a book to read, nor do you have headphones. You stare out the window as dark Melbourne suburbia rolls on into shops as you get closer in.

"Sophie?" you hear a familiar male voice ask. You turn to look at him and smile as he sits opposite you.

Why couldn't he pretend he hadn't seen me? You ask yourself.

"Hi James," you say, repressing the urge to call him babe. You broke up six months ago, but you still want to say it. "How've you been?"

"Oh, you know, getting up to this and that." He grins and there is a little flutter in your stomach as he looks you up and down. "You look fabulous, babe, what's on the cards tonight?"

"Felicity has twisted my arm to go with her to a party at South Wharf, I think there was mention of a boat. I don't really remember." You can feel yourself grinning back at him. "Apparently she would have literally died had I allowed her to go alone."

"Really? We can't have that! And your boyfriend lets you go out looking like that? Alone?"

You giggle involuntarily. James has complimented your outfit and is now shamelessly trying to work out if you're seeing anyone. You shouldn't encourage him, it can't possibly end well. James Bryon is as charming as he is dangerous.

"I'm not seeing anyone just now and I don't need chaperoning, thank you very much." You watch him carefully, he raises an eyebrow, and his eyes twinkle a little more mischievously.

"And where are you off to, mister? All dressed up…" you say as you take in his highly polished black patent leather shoes, the ones he hates because they're uncomfortable. They're the going out shoes he wears to impress. Coupled with the seersucker suit, black waistcoat and crisp black tie, he's definitely going somewhere special.

He tugs on the hem of the waistcoat; it's an unconscious preening movement you've seen before. "The same place as you, my dear. I've been told it's going to be quite a to-do." He's smiling again, the one he knows you can't resist.

Looking back out the dark windows, you start searching your memories for why you and James split up. It's the only thing that will stop you from falling back in love with him. He's so close you can smell his cologne. It was never the attraction that was the problem between you; it was the fact that it was not only you he was attracted to. A seed of pain and betrayal grows in your chest, helping to counteract your body's automatic arousal at his unique aroma.

James spends most of the tram ride telling you about his work. You feed him questions each time it looks like he's running out of material and keep him on safe topics.

*

The party turns out to be huge, you can hear it from at least a hundred metres away, the pounding bass beat throbbing through the night air.

James walks you in, taking your hand and placing it in the crook of his arm. His fancy suit has apparently brought out the theatrical in him. Once inside the converted warehouse, you see a rabbit warren of corridors and small rooms, all filled with bodies. You and James walk through several rooms heading towards the source of the music and come out into a vast open space.

The stage is at one end, with a small group of people dancing in front of it. There is a DJ playing, he seems small standing alone on the stage hiding behind his decks. At the back of the room, there are high tables and a couple of bar stools. One section of the room is enclosed by a white picket fence with a mini dance floor and seating.

"The VIP area I presume," James leans close to your ear to speak over the music. You can feel his breath on your skin.

"Very exclusive, I'm sure," you reply.

Across the room you see Felicity.

CHOOSE:

If you ditch James and go to greet Felicity, go to <u>p 155</u>.

If you take James with you to greet Felicity, go to <u>p 174</u>.

C1.2.1 O1 You chose to ditch James and go to greet Felicity…

You disengage your arm from James as you trot over to greet your best friend.

"Was that James? The famously terrible awful no-good ex of yours whose arm you were on?" Felicity says, frowning at you.

You feel your face heat up with a blush. "Yes, he was on my tram. I tried to be strong but he's got his charming face on tonight. And he smells so gooood."

"You definitely should not be smelling him!" she says.

"I know. That's why I came over to you as soon as I saw you. I will be strong."

"You'd better be. I don't want to have to nurse your through the aftermath of that again!"

"Please, remind me! I forget everything when he's right there. Let's get a drink before he comes over," you say, spotting a bar behind Felicity.

Now that you're out of the immediate sphere of James' physical presence it is much easier to remember what he did to you.

Felicity's new crush is just arriving as you make you way back through the swarm of people at the bar. She told you about him, but she could never do justice to the way he carried himself. Tall, broad-shouldered with unruly golden curls he looks like he should be in a Renaissance painting.

"So are we going over?" you ask, taking a sip of the delightfully sour cocktail.

Felicity turns to you, her face scrunched up with exaggerated anxiety.

"Come on then." You grab her hand and make your way to the enormous cherub and his friend.

"Eric!" Felicity grabs him into a hug as she come to them, he responds by whispering something in her ear as his hug lifts her off the ground. His name reminds you of a Viking King, and perhaps he could be a Viking if not for the curls; they make his face angelic rather than rugged, even with the strong jaw.

"This is my friend, Sophie," Felicity introduces you to the two of them, "Sophie this is Eric and his friend Tom. They went to school together, didn't you?"

"Uni actually," Tom replies, holding out his hands towards you. You expect him to go for a handshake but he leans in and hugs you, you feel his body under his suit is toned and lean. You take a little too long to let him go.

Settle down girl! you tell yourself silently. It's James' fault for getting you all excited, now you're sizing up any male in the immediate radius.

Tom is very attentive to your conversation and you find you enjoy his company immensely. The four of you find a spot in one of the quieter rooms to sit down, pushing thoughts of James from your brain.

"We're going to the bar, you need another one?" Felicity asks, holding Eric's hand as they stand up.

"Yes please." You realise that you have been holding your empty glass and hand it to her. "Take my purse with you, babe, you got the last round."

Felicity leans down towards you, still holding Eric's hand, "Eric's shout, don't worry about it." You look up and he nods, then turns to Tom and mimes drinking and gives a thumbs up. Tom gives a thumbs up back from beside you.

As Felicity and Eric walk away to find a bar Tom shifts his position on the couch. You can feel his thigh pressing against yours. Your dress has ridden up and most of your thigh is naked against his suit. It feels naughty to enjoy pressing against him like that, you're sure he isn't the least bit interested in you.

"Do you think your friend has figured out Eric is into her yet?" Tom asks.

"I should hope so, I would have thought that the hand holding was a dead giveaway of a fellow's interest."

Tom drops his eyes to your hand, resting on your bared thigh, and lays his own hand on top of it.

"Like this, you mean?" He brings his eyes up to meet yours, while curling his fingers around your hand, brushing his fingertips across your inner thigh as he does so.

You can seem to find any words to respond, so you focus on breathing in and out, steadily, fighting your sudden breathlessness.

Tom leans over and kisses you gently on the mouth. His skin is smooth and soft, freshly shaved, he smells like subtle woody cologne and a little bit like soap, and tastes of citrus and beer. He kisses you tenderly, your bodies only linked at the lips and hands. You let out a small sigh as he pulls away and when you flutter open your eyes he's staring at you intensely.

"How was that?" he asks.

"I don't know. I think you need to try it again, just to be sure." You smile at him and lean forward to meet him. He's more urgent now, so are you, you twist your knees towards him and he slips a hand between your thighs. Instinctively you tense and clamp his hand where it is, but as the two of you kiss, you relax.

Tom leaves his hand where it is. You want this, and you want him to know that, so you take hold of his upper arms and squeeze them, drawing him towards you and forcing his hand further up your leg.

He pulls back and looks around, you assume he's looking for Flick and Eric with the drinks.

"I think they must have gotten distracted," he says.

"Where were we?" You lean towards him again, your desire for sex is now all you can think about.

"I'm not looking for anything, y' know, relationship wise, right now. I just wanted to know what it was like to kiss you."

"Oh, ok, well, umm, so you're just after a hook up?" You want to clarify what's on offer even though your brain is filled with images of fucking him.

CHOOSE:

If you say yes and go home with Tom, go to p 159.

If you say no and decide to call it a night, go to p 163.

C1.2.2 O1 You chose to go home with Tom…

"Yes, I just wanted to be clear with you before, we, uh, got too far down the…track."

His hand is still between your legs, his fingertips only centimetres away from your underwear. You're sure he can feel the heat coming off your groin.

"I appreciate it, I'm not really looking for anything either," you lie, partly to Tom and partly to yourself. "But I am having fun, so, why stop now right?"

"Right!" He kisses you hard on the mouth and reaches his other arm around your waist, gripping you tightly.

"So, you wanna get out of here?" you ask.

"I was thinking about finding a quiet corner. I'm so bad." His palm is now pressing against the fabric of your underwear.

"Do you know a spot?" you say, you breath coming in short, shallow grasps.

"Follow me." He wriggles his eyebrows and pulls you up off the couch and along behind him.

You push your way through hundreds of people in various states of inebriation as Tom leads you out of the building and into the cold night air. The cold brings you back into your mind and you wonder if you've had enough alcohol to make this a good idea.

Sophie's Path

Just as you're thinking about changing your mind and going back to the party Tom swings you around and grabs you roughly in a full body embrace. With his mouth on yours, his smell in your nostrils and the hardness of his cock pressed against you. You forget all of your misgivings.

You run your hands all over him, feeling the silky fabric sliding under your fingers. He moves with you until you are leaning against a cold wall; the contrast of the coolness of your back and the fire where you're touching him causes you to gasp.

His hand is up inside your skirt again, his fingers stroking your underwear.

"God, you're so wet," he says.

"I know. I want you so badly." You thrust your hand down the front of his pants and brush your knuckles over his hard cock; you feel him shudder with excitement.

He pushes your underwear aside and slips two fingers inside you. You moan softly, throwing your head back.

Almost instantly he has released himself from his pants and is tearing the condom wrapper with his teeth.

"Let me," you say, taking it from him, so that he can leave his other and where it is.

When you have the condom securely in place Tom lifts you up against the wall and slides himself in where his fingers have been.

You wrap your arms and legs around him, willing him to be deeper, to be more a part of you. He responds by pushing his whole bodyweight against you.

Tom's thrusts are quick and powerful, you can feel yourself gliding towards your climax, when he shudders and grunts. You know that he's come, and he slows to a stop, still pinning you to the wall but shaking a little now.

"Hmm, God, I needed that," he says, lowering you to the ground as he pulls away. You can feel your arousal slowly fading, unsatisfied. Knowing that you'll never get to try again makes it worse somehow, if that was as good as it gets you wonder if it would have been better to have said no.

"I'm going back inside," he says, zipping his fly and flicking the used condom behind the skip which you didn't see before. "You coming?"

You feel cold, slimy and you're disappointed in yourself. You should have seen this when he said he wanted to hook up.

"No, I'm going to get a cab home."

"Okay, I'll walk with you to the front."

Tom is distant now; he walks beside you but leaves a gap as though you barely know each other. Only minutes ago he was part of you, now you don't know if he even remembers your name.

When you reach the road you don't want him to stand with you any more, he's obviously itching to get back into the party. Maybe he wants to see if he can find someone else to take into the alley, you think.

"I'll be alright from here, thanks," you say.

"It was nice to meet you."

"Yeah, you too."

You both stand there for what feels like a long time, not sure whether to give him a hug, or a kiss, or shake his hand. In the end you do none of these and he turns to go back into the party.

You have failed in your mission, go back to the beginning and try again.

C1.2.2 O2 You chose to call it a night…

You take a moment to think about what Tom is saying. You reach down and take his hand from between your thighs.

"I don't really like hook ups. Sorry."

Tom lowers his eyes and sighs. "It's always a possibility when I say these things that I'll get a no, but not very often." He lifts his eyes and smiles at you, although he seems sad.

"Is Eric on the same wavelength as you?" you ask, as you remember the way he and Felicity left, what seems like hours ago, but was probably only a few minutes.

"Nah, he's looking for lurve, apparently. He's not like me. Your friend's heart is safe."

"I didn't mean…." You falter. You did mean to insinuate that you were worried about Flick's feelings, but you didn't intend to hurt Tom in the process. "I'm glad you told me, it's important to be up front, but now I'm feeling quite confused and I don't trust myself to make the same choice in an hour after a few more drinks. I gonna head home."

"No worries," he says, some of the energy coming back into his face and voice. You suppose a man like Tom doesn't dwell on rejection too much.

"I'll leave you to it, then, I doubt I'll see the other two on the way out, so if you see them before I do, let them know I went home."

"Sure thing." He leans over to kiss you once more, gently and chastely on the lips.

Sophie's Path

You peel yourself off the vinyl-covered couch and make you way through the crowded rooms towards the street. You glance at your phone, it's only 11:30 p.m, you might even be able to get the tram home.

Not feeling it tonight, babe, heading home. Hope you and Eric are having fun ;) You text Felicity, knowing she probably won't see it until later, but feeling as though you should make an effort to tell her anyway.

As you walk through the last rabbit warren-like room on the way to the doors, you spot James standing in a corner with a voluptuous woman. He's leaning down to speak in her ear and she's giggling, by the way she's almost sliding sideways down the wall you suspect she's far too drunk to know what she's doing. You want to give James the benefit of the doubt, but you know he's keeping her drinks topped up and will probably take her home.

Good thing you didn't fall into his trap, you think as you approach the tram stop. You have fifteen minutes to wait and you go into your mobile phone contacts list and change James contact to "Do Not Call James Byron". Maybe it will stop you from calling him some time in the future.

*

The morning after you wake up feeling better than you expected. Going home relatively early and not having had much to drink clearly agrees with you. You look over and find that it's just after nine o'clock.

Felicity won't be awake yet, but you check your phone to see whether she's replied. Nothing. Maybe she got lucky with Eric; that would be a good reason not to reply, you think with a smile.

Your mind wanders to Tom and to how nice you felt under the attention of an attractive man. Maybe you're ready to start thinking about dating again. James is still a temptation but perhaps having someone else to pour your time and affection into would make it easier the next time you see him on the tram or at a party.

Since you're feeling so spritely you go for a long walk and treat yourself to brunch and coffee at the place down the road.

"Hi Brett, how's things?" you say as you enter.

"Not bad, thanks love, run off me feet as usual, but I always have time for you." Brett has a thick working class English accent. He's told you before what region of England he grew up in, but you've forgotten and you're too shy to ask again.

"Looks pretty busy, any spots?"

"Lemme have a look, love." Brett moves around the tightly packed café and then turns to beckon you over. Brett leads you through the narrow café and into the courtyard outside. There is cloth strung between the building and the fence creating shade and lush green plants in pots attached to the wall. Every table is occupied and you aren't sure where you're supposed to sit.

"Here you go, love. Sorry I haven't got a table for you, but you can sit here with Alfred, he's a nice sort of fella," Brett says with a grin, teasing Alfred you suspect.

"Thanks, that'll be fine," you say as Brett walks away.

You sit down opposite Alfred, a very serious-looking man of about thirty. He has glasses, stubble and rich, brown hair which flops down over his forehead when he moves.

"I'm Sophie." You extend your hand across the table, "it's nice to meet you, if somewhat awkward."

"Pleased to meet you too, Sophie, Sophie, Sophie. I tend to find repeating people's names makes me more likely to remember them, Sophie, so I promise I'm not a weirdo, Sophie."

When he smiles, Alfred's whole face lights up. Suddenly the serious intensity melts away and he looks carefree and joyous.

"And call me Freddie, only people at work call me Alfred. And pricks like Brett." He smiles as he says it, part of the masculine teasing routine, you guess.

"Alright, Freddie. What do you do for work?"

He takes a sip from his coffee, a long black, and studies you before answering. "What do you think I do?" he asks, his head cocked to the side.

You sit back in your seat and fold your arms over your chest. "Let me see. You're brunching alone on a Saturday morning, so not retail or hospitality. And your hands are clean and smooth, not a manual job, so an office job then."

You pause and watch his smiling face; he nods to you to continue.

"Office job can mean a lot of things though. I don't think you work in sales or customer service, but maybe you're in the more operational side of things...I'm going to guess actuary."

He laughs quietly. "I like your methodical inductive reasoning, but unfortunately incorrect. I work in the office of a politician, so a sort of jack-of-all-trades aide to the MP."

"That sounds…do you like your job?" You aren't quite sure how to react as he hasn't told you which politician. It seems grown up but also light on details. You have no clues about what he actually does all day.

"It's okay. I don't think I'll be doing it forever, but it's definitely interesting."

Brett comes over to take your order, and you and Freddie continue to chat. It's mostly surface level stuff and you find yourself becoming comfortable in his presence.

Finally, once your breakfasts are cleared away and you've finished your second coffee, Freddie looks at his watch.

"I'm so sorry Sophie, I have things I have to do. There's a barbeque event at the MPs office tomorrow that I have to get organised. So much for the idea I don't work weekends," he winks at you. "It was lovely talking to you, perhaps we'll see each other again?"

You feel a sudden stab of anxiety deep in your belly. This can't be last you see of him.

"Have you got a card or something? Maybe we could have brunch again sometime?"

Your heart is pounding in your chest. You never ask for a number. The suggestion is out there in the world now and all you can do is hope that he is keen. You haven't managed to ask him whether he's seeing anyone, and it didn't come up. It might have seemed mercenary on your first meeting.

"I…" he pats his back pocket. "I don't have one with me. How about I give you my mobile number and we can work something out."

You grin back at him. "Lovely. Perfect." You flip over the paper napkin on the table and he somehow produces a pen from somewhere.

"There we go," he says as he hands you the number and stands up. "I really must dash, see you soon I hope." He bends down to give you a peck on the cheek before he turns to leave.

You look down at your walking outfit, and wonder what he could have possible seen in you to say yes; no makeup, slightly sweaty, and wearing a decidedly unflattering baggy T-shirt and leggings. It must have been something you said, you think.

You catch yourself grinning all day. You decide that you can't text him until after it's dark, otherwise it might be considered too soon. You usually try not to get too wrapped up in that sort of stuff, how long to wait before calling someone, but you don't want to seem like a stalker.

"Hi Freddie, this is Sophie, from brunch. I hope you got whatever you needed to do done. When would suit you to catch up?"

You feel like a bit of an idiot, you agonised over what to write for a good twenty minutes before giving up and just sending the next thing that came into your head.

He doesn't reply immediately and you decide to put your phone in the bedroom and watch T.V. to distract yourself.

You end up falling asleep on the couch and you're woken by the sound of your alarm drifting in from the bedroom. When you get up you realise that you're back is really stiff from the peculiar position you slept in and you have to rush through the shower.

You get to work late and Candace is waiting impatiently for you to arrive.

"Sophie, don't you know we've got to get over to see Telstra today?" she says grabbing your arm as you walk past and turning you both back towards the lifts.

"Shit, shit, I'm so sorry I completely forgot. I don't know where my head is this morning."

"I've called them to say we've been held up but it really isn't a good look."

"I know, I had a bit of a rough night. I think I'm coming down with something," you say, knowing it's a lie. Candace seems placated.

During the meeting with Telstra you keep thinking about Freddie, who still hasn't replied. You miss an important cue from Candace and have to apologise profusely again.

"Maybe you are coming down with something. You look a bit, grey." She touches the back of her hand to your forehead.

"A good night's sleep and I should be fine for tomorrow."

Freddie finally replies at midnight on Monday.

"Great chat yesterday. Super hectic. Weekend would be good. Or Friday night?"

You see the message as you wake up on Tuesday morning while you're still feeling stiff and groggy with sleep. At least he gave you the right number, you think.

Friday night... could have drinks after work? Maybe grab some food if we're feeling excited. You send back from the tram in to work. It's a struggle to concentrate all day at work and you wonder if you really are coming down with something.

Sophie's Path

*

In the Wednesday meeting Aubrey stands up to make an announcement.

"I have some exciting news. You might be aware that I've been in discussion with a chain of medium-sized hotels all over Australia. We've just signed an agreement to open a new site in Mackay for which I have promised to provide an employee, full-time for six months, to help get things going. So I'm asking for applications for anyone who might be interested in the position. The details are yet to be finalised, but obviously we would get together a good package, accommodation paid for and an allowance for being away from home. The deadline for expressions of interest is close of business on Friday. Thanks for your time, see you all next week."

There are low mutterings as the staff start to leave the meeting room.

"I know you haven't been feeling well the last few days, but Aubrey mentioned to me earlier he specifically wants to see your application for this project," Candace says to you.

"I wasn't really thinking of applying, it's not really something I've ever thought I would do," you say. You've never considered moving away from the hub of Melbourne.

"Why not? It'd be fantastic exposure. Your career would be set for the next five, even ten years if you did well at it."

Candace hurries off after Aubrey and you're left feeling unheard and flustered. It's not her fault that she misinterpreted your objection, but for some reason you feel even more determined to stay in Melbourne now.

Fleur Blūm

*

By Friday you're feeling decidedly seedy but determined to keep your date with Freddie. You dress yourself in your finest, most daring work appropriate outfit to meet him for drinks after work.

"It's so nice to see you again," you say as he walks into the bar you chose not far from your offices. It's down a flight of stairs from street level and the interior is painted a lush forest green. You've settled yourself into a booth in the corner so that you can watch the door.

"Of course! I've been looking forward to this all week. It's been super hectic!" He leans forward to give you a kiss on the cheek and you try to give him a hug. There is an awkward moment of indecision, but you end up laughing a little and doing both.

"Can I buy you a drink?" Freddie says, giving you his elbow before he leads you to the bar.

"That sounds wonderful," you reply.

"I feel like red wine, why don't I splash out and get a nice bottle?" Freddie says.

"Yes, why not! I don't know anything about wine really, except obviously, red and white are like different colours," you say.

The waiter brings the bottle over to the darkened booth as you settle in. Freddie sits across the table from you.

He smiles, that enigmatic smile which changes the whole structure of his face. If he looked like that all the time you would do just about anything he asked.

When Freddie offers to top up your glass for the third time you're starting to feel very sleepy and a little bit drunk. He he's moved his way around the booth to be next to you, his thigh pressing against yours.

He places the bottle on the table carefully. You can't seem to tear your eyes away from the places where your bodies touch.

Freddie reaches his hand out to your knee and you drag your eyes up to look at his face. He's so close to you that you can feel his warm breath on your neck.

He smells delicious, the chocolaty undertones of the wine along with the dry fruitiness of his cologne are delicious. You want to put him into your mouth and taste him.

You lean forward and kiss him. He pulls away slightly in surprise, but soon he's pushing back, kissing you back forcefully, urgently.

After a few minutes it occurs to you that you're in a public place and you turn your head towards his shoulder.

"We're making a spectacle of ourselves," you whisper.

"Should we stop?" he asks.

"Yes. Probably." You turn to kiss him again.

"We should stop," he says, breathlessly. "We could go somewhere else though, like, uh, my house, uh, if you want to continue…"

You give Freddie a quick peck on the lips. "Why not?"

Grabbing his hand, you pull him up and in minutes you're both in the back of a taxi heading for his place. He lives only minutes from your place and you are surprised by the fact that a man so gorgeous, generous, lovely, and just what you're looking for was living around the corner and you didn't even know it.

Fleur Blüm

You and Freddie make a lovely couple.
The End.

C1.2.1 O2 You chose take James with you to greet Felicity…

You wave to her and grab James's hand, dragging him behind you to say hello to Felicity.

As soon as she sees who you're approaching with, she narrows her eyes in disapproval.

"Hello, James." Felicity stands with her arms folded across her chest. She turns to you giving you an exaggerated air-kiss. "You look fab, darling, where did you find this one?"

"We were on the same tram and we were both coming here, isn't that wild?" you say. You're struggling to remain composed under Felicity's angry gaze.

"Yes. Wild," she replies, refolding her arms. "James, be a dear and get us some drinks would you?" She thrusts some money into his hand as she gives him a little shove in the direction of the bar.

"That was a bit rude, wasn't it?" you say once James is out of earshot.

"I'm a bit much? Have you seen who you came in with? James Fucking Byron. The two-faced snake who ripped your still beating heart out of your chest, threw it on the floor and pissed on it. Or have you forgotten? You need to get rid of him. Now."

You clench your jaw. Felicity's tone is totally uncalled for. Yes, the two of you had a somewhat messy breakup, but you're not getting back together, you're just being friendly.

"Yes. I know what happened, I'm not likely to ever forget it. I'm just trying to be civil. There's no need for us to completely avoid each other, we have similar circles of friends, it's bound to happen."

"Civil is one thing, but the star-struck-puppy-dog-look in your eye and the flush in your cheeks are taking it a bit further than civil." She raises an eyebrow at you.

You bring the back of your hand up to feel your face. Dammit, it's warm, you think. Maybe she's right.

James makes his way back towards you with three glasses of champagne.

"Ladies," he says as he hands them out. "I'm so surprised to see you here, babe. I wouldn't have thought it was your deal." James directs his last comment to you.

Felicity rolls her shoulders back and puffs her chest out, as though she's getting ready for a fight.

"It's really none of your concern what is and isn't her 'deal', or mine for that matter," she says. She turns to glares at you before she continues. "I'm going to see if I can find Eric, are you coming?"

You know that if you don't move away from James, your attraction will take over and your memories of past pain will not be enough to stop you doing something very stupid.

"I need to meet this Eric person. Sorry, James, maybe we can catch up later on."

"Definitely," he replies, as he leans over to give you a kiss on the cheek. He lingers longer than strictly necessary and you breathe in his familiar scent.

He knows exactly what he's doing, you think as you pull away and follow Felicity. She's already started across the room towards the rabbit warren-like back section of the warehouse.

Sophie's Path

You squeeze your way through the other party goers as quickly as you can to try to catch up with Felicity who is clearing a path in front of her with the anger she's exuding. You're surprised by how badly she reacted to the situation, it's not like her to be so moody. Maybe it's nerves about Eric, you think.

Felicity is walking into a third smaller chill out room when you catch up to her, you can feel waves of cold anger coming off her.

"Eric!" she squeals as she rushes over to a tall muscular man, jumping up to hug him. As he bends to say hello, his curly blond hair tumbles across his eyes, he swings it away with a toss of his head as he looks back up to you.

"And who's this charming lady?" he asks her.

"This is my best friend in the whole world Sophie. Sophie, this is Eric."

"Hi," you say, reaching out to shake his hand.

"C'mon now, I've heard a lot about you, let's have a hug." He holds his arms wide and you allow him to embrace you. It's a very nice hug but your senses are still filled with James.

"This is Tom," Eric indicates to another very handsome man sitting on a hay bale covered in khaki-coloured canvas behind him.

"Hi Tom," you say. "I wore very silly shoes, so I'm ready to have a little sit down" With your mind now clearing of James, your feet remind you of the sprint to the tram earlier.

"Well, it's not as comfy as it looks but better than standing in silly shoes." His gaze sweeps you up and down in a cocky wolfish manner. "Although they are very nice shoes."

Felicity drains her champagne and looks at you, "Eric and I are going to the bar, you want anything?"

Your champagne is still almost full. "I'll have whatever you're having, do you want my purse?"

"Nah, we'll get this one, you get the next one," she replies, while her eyes flit between you and Tom, in what you assume is intended suggest you should pursue him.

The hay bale beside Tom is strangely lumpy and stiff.

"Ergh, you weren't wrong," you smile at him and slide your feet out of the shoes. "So, uh," you start to say, but falter as Tom, at the same time, says, "how did you hear about this gig?"

You become aware of how close his leg is to yours and that he doesn't seem to be inclined at all to move, "I'm just here because Felicity asked me."

"Eric is quite taken with her, you know."

"Is he? I'm glad, she's been super anxious about him."

"Well, she's definitely in safe hands there."

Neither of you say anything, the time stretches out and you feel pressure to say something interesting.

From where you are sitting you see Felicity standing at the bar leaning on Eric's shoulder. The four drinks they bought for you are in front of her, but it doesn't look like she'll be coming over any time soon.

You fidget with your skirt hem, which rode up when you sat down, and finish your champagne. When you look over to Tom he's happily grooving to the thundering music, clearly he isn't concerned by the lack of conversation.

Eric and Felicity are now locking lips next to the bar causing congestion in the line for drinks, to which they're oblivious. On the other side of the room you see

James lurking, your eyes lock and you look away instantly, and your gaze lands on Tom's lap.

CHOOSE:

If you decide to ignore James and try to get Tom talking, go to p 179.

If you excuse yourself from Tom and go talk to James, go to p 190.

C1.2.3 O1 You chose to ignore James and try to get Tom talking...

You look up and realise Tom has seen you staring at his groin. Heat rushes into your cheeks.

"Sorry, I just saw my ex and I was trying to avoid him, he's over there by the door." You wave your hand in James's direction without looking over. "We got chatting on the way in and I think he's trying to seduce me."

He doesn't need to know all this, just reel it in, you tell yourself. "It's all a bit much, we had a terrible breakup and it wasn't that long ago and I'm starting to worry there are unresolved feelings, y' know, sorry, I'm babbling." You couldn't stop yourself, perhaps it's the champagne. You put your hand over your face and take a deep breath.

Tom reaches up and gently pulls your hand away from your eyes.

"It's okay. No need to be embarrassed, we all have exes. Sounds like he's being a total weirdo. They can just walk back into your life whenever it suits them. Let's go get our drinks."

He takes your hand and helps you back onto your giant, ridiculous, gorgeous shoes. He keeps hold of your hand as you move over toward the bar.

"Do you think he saw? I was hoping it would send a message." Tom says as you reach the others and he lets go of your hand.

"I'm sure he did. Thank you." You feel strangely grateful to Tom, and you wonder whether he might be trying to seduce you too, in his way.

Get a grip, not everyone wants to sleep with you, you think.

Tom hovers near your shoulder and Eric and Felicity keep getting distracted by kissing each other. The bass thump is starting to give you a headache and you're worried that James is going to come back lurking and looking for you.

You glance at your phone to check the time, it's approaching midnight, not that late for this sort of party but it's later than you've been out for some time.

"I think I'm going to head home," you tell Felicity in one of the few moments she is not conjoined to Eric.

"Okay, babe," she gives you a peck on the cheek and a one-armed hug. She smells like men's cologne.

"Text me when you get home. We can do brunch maybe tomorrow," you say as you turn to leave.

"You going already?" Tom asks.

"I'm tired and it's not really my scene, I just came to be company for Flick."

Tom smiles. "Well, it was very nice to meet you, perhaps well be seeing each other a bit more in the future." He winks and hugs you tightly, rubbing your back in an overly familiar way. You try not to flinch, he's probably just being friendly.

You pull away from the embrace and hurry towards the exit. Outside you hail a taxi, and sitting alone in the back you decide to get McDonald's on the way home.

*

The next morning you get up early and go for a nice long walk. You listen to your favourite music and have to stop yourself from singing along a couple of times. You've never been a particularly good singer, but you are enthusiastic, sometimes at inopportune times.

While you're halfway up a big hill about to head into the home stretch your mum calls. You briefly debate answering it but decide that you deserve the little rest.

"Hi, Mum," you say, breathing heavily.

"Oh, hi darl, have I caught you at a bad time? I can call back."

"No, no, it's fine. I'm out for a walk."

"Righto. I was just calling to see if you can come round today sometime, I need you to help with my iPad. I can't seem to get my emails to work. I'll make something yummy for dinner if you like."

"Yeah, alright. I can come for dinner."

"Good, good…"

"I better get back to this walk before I lose motivation. I'll see you later." You hang up the phone and march the rest of the way home.

You love your mum but you can't help feeling. You know she can work the iPad without any trouble but she always likes to have a reason to invite you over.

Back home you shower briefly and settle in to reading a book. You wait until six to head to your mum's place. She drives you mad if you stay too long in her house, but in small doses she can be lovely.

Her place is a twenty minute drive down the freeway towards the south-east. She has a two bedroom cottage with a little garden in the front where she grows vegies, and a courtyard out the back where she sits with her coffee in the morning.

"Oh, there you are!" she says as she opens the door. You have a key but you like to knock anyway. "I thought you weren't coming."

"I said I was coming, didn't I?" You sigh.

It's the same every time you see her, you've never stood her up but she gets worried when you're even two minutes behind when she thinks you'll be there.

You follow her down the narrow hallway in your socks. She's recently bought new carpets and no longer allows shoes indoors. You settle in the small kitchen and sit at the tiny table. She grabs the iPad and holds it out to you.

"Well, you're here now. Can you fix the emails for me?"

"Okay." You take the device and swipe it to the right. Your mother leans back against the stove watching you intently.

You go into her emails and instead of updating, it asks you for the password.

"What's your password mum?"

She tells you and you type it in.

"That's not it."

She thinks for a moment before giving you a different one.

"Yeah that works. That should be fixed now." You hand it back to her.

"Thank you, baby. You know how lost I would be without you." She trots over and kisses the top of your head, taking the iPad and sliding it into a drawer.

It takes all of your will power not to roll your eyes. "It's okay."

The two of you eat shrivelled lamb chops and steamed vegies as your mother tells your all about her friends, and her friends' children. You know that it's important for her to tell you this stuff but you really don't care that much. Sometimes it occurs to you that she mustn't have many people to talk to, the way she launches into hugely detailed monologues whenever you visit.

You don't have to pay too much attention to keep her going; occasionally throwing in a question to show you're listening. It's about nine o'clock when you decide you'd better head home.

"I've got work tomorrow. Is there anything that needs doing before I go?"

"No, nothing I can think of." She smiles at you; her eyes look watery and faraway.

"Alright, well, I'll see you around." You stand up and give her a hug before retreating back to your car.

She stands at the front door waving to you as you drive away. It makes you sad to see your mum so lonely and you decide you're going to start trying to get her to meet someone. Not that you necessarily want her to remarry, but a bit of attention, someone to spent time with, to make her feel nice, feminine, would make such a difference in her life.

As you pass the golden arches on the way home you think about stopping for some chips, but you decide against it. You had Maccas last night you remind yourself.

*

Felicity drops in for lunch while you're at work on Tuesday and you head to a little Japanese cafe not far from your office. The chairs are so low and hard your butt is always sore, but their sushi rolls are the best value around.

She's full of boasting about Eric who she went home with after the warehouse party.

"He's…let's just say, he's not small, and certainly knows what he's going."

"Oh God, I don't want to know!" You smile, you're pretending jealousy but there's a grain of truth in it. You've haven't been single that long, but given the way it all went so wrong with James, you feel like it's been a long time since anyone loved and cared you.

"I'm sorry, I know I'm just rubbing it in. But it's exciting, y' know, want to share it with my best friend."

"I know." You take her hand across the table and squeeze it. "Hey, what do you think of his friend, Tom? There were a few, flirtatious moments on Saturday night."

"Oh, Tom? Hmm." Felicity pauses thoughtfully. "I haven't met him before, and he seems nice, but I don't know. Eric didn't have completely great things to say about him."

"Really? Do tell." You try to sound excited for the goss, but you can't help feeling the tendril of hope you had for something with him die inside you.

"Well, Eric says he hasn't managed to hold onto a women since uni, I had the same thought you did, I saw what was going on," she says.

You're surprised that she saw anything outside of Eric. Perhaps her mind isn't as one-track as you think.

"Don't look so shocked, you were hardly subtle," she says. "Anyway, Eric reckons he's only looking for hookups so I wouldn't…I mean, unless that's what you want."

"Nah, I'm not really good with that sort of thing."

Inside your chest the lonely ache begins to swell. You fight it back, now isn't the time to be wallowing in self-pity. You realise that Felicity has stopped talking and is staring at you.

"You'll find someone. I know it's hard, after what that fucking bastard did, but not all men are like that. You're a beautiful, strong, intelligent woman, you just need to meet the right guy and you'll get your happily ever after."

The tears that you're barely managing to suppress threaten to break their way through and you just nod. You're sure that if you talked you'd cry.

Felicity squeezes your hand. You sit together holding hands quietly for a long moment.

"Damn, I have to run back to work. Thanks for lunch, Flick, I want to hear more about this Eric next time!" you say as you realise the time.

She smiles back at you. "Just try and stop me!"

*

Back at your desk there is a post-it note from your old boss.

Come see me ASAP–Max.

You walk through the open plan office towards Max's office. Since leaving his team about six months ago to go into client liaison Max has been a bit of a mentor for you. He's a more experienced, but somewhat removed person, who you can turn to for advice.

"Sophie, good. Sit down."

"Hey, what's up?" you ask cheerfully, but Max's solemn face cause your smile to fall from your face.

"Well, there's been some, uh, anomalies, found in the payroll system and they've been traced back to Candace. Thousands of dollars have been misappropriated since she'd been here. They've suspended her with pay while they figure out whether it really was her and what they need to do if it was."

"What? Candace? I would not have expected that from her," you say.

"Everyone on the executive was floored when Calvin suggested that the anomalies came from her, but he had the paper trail. There's going to be a full investigation, obviously, but they need someone to lead the team while she's off. Aubrey wanted me to put it to you."

"Me? But..." you can't quite wrap your mind around the situation. "I've only just joined the department, how can I possibly lead them?"

"You were a team leader with me. You know how to handle people. You don't need to be an expert in clients or sales to manage the team. It's only an interim measure, obviously, but I think you would be wise to take advantage of it."

You sit for a moment considering the idea. You're confident in your skills as a team leader, you had three staff reporting to you with Max, but this is a new department, a new group of people.

"There's eight people in Candace's team. Well, seven without me. That's a big step up. I only had three with you."

"I know. We're aware and you would be given an appropriate higher duties allowance for taking on the extra work and responsibility." He watches you from his round, serious, fatherly face.

"No one expects miracle from you. Mainly we need you to stop the team from self-destructing during the investigation. If it turns out the accusations are true, they'd want you to keep managing until they found a permanent replacement."

"Right." It hadn't occurred to you that Candace's job was on the line, although it makes sense. Defrauding the company is serious, and getting fired is definitely a valid punishment, but it's so unlike Candace it doesn't seem real that she could be fired.

"I'll give it a go. I mean, I can't promise anything, I really have no idea what I'm doing but..." You realise you haven't seen Candace all day. "Is she banned from the office?"

"When the evidence came through that the breaches were from her, she was asked to leave the office. We still need to follow the procedure, of course, and you can't say anything about this to anyone, but she needed to be out of the building just in case she was trying to cover her tracks," Max says.

"Jesus." You stare at the wall behind Max's head.

"It's all a bit unbelievable, I know. I'm getting everything I can together for you so that you can learn the job as you go. Aubrey will be your direct superior now, and of course you can come to me for anything. I haven't ever done the job, but I've been here a long time so I know a few tricks. Aubrey is happy for you to ask him anything, but with his schedule it might be tricky."

"Thanks," you say.

You're mind is spinning with the size of the shift in your life over the space of a few minutes.

Max sends all the information he's collected to you in an email. You try to read through it but you can't make much sense of it. You get up to make yourself a cup of tea and walk past the closed door of Candace's office.

"What's this about you acting for Candace while she's on leave?" Jenny, one of the staff you know supervise, asks as you're standing at the kitchen bench jiggle your tea bag.

"Hey?" you say.

"An email's just come through from Aubrey saying you're in charge of the department effective immediately and that Candace has had to take leave suddenly. As if you didn't know." Jenny's crossed her arms across her chest and has a scrunch to her mouth that you don't much like.

You have no idea what Aubrey has put in that email, so you chose your words carefully. "I only just heard about it myself. They haven't told me much more than they've told you, but that Candace is off for the moment and they want me to fill in if I can."

"This is bullshit," Jenny says. "You've only just got here. What makes Aubrey think he can just put you in charge of people who are much more experienced than you?"

"Well, I was a team leader over in Analysis, and I guess since it's only temporary I just have to keep the wheels on this train till Candace is back. As long as I have experienced people like you to help me, I think it will be fine."

Jenny looked frowns. "I guess there's no use complaining."

She stalks back to her desk and you know you're going to have to keep your eye on her.

After four weeks the investigation is over and the company is confident that they can support a claim that Candace had embezzled funds and she's fired. When they advertise her role you apply. Based on good performance in the Acting Manager role you get the job. Well done.

The End.

C1.2.3 O2 You chose to excuse yourself from Tom and go talk to James...

The twinge of guilt you felt at ditching James earlier comes back into your gut.

"I'm just going over to say hello to someone, tell Felicity I won't be long if she comes back before me, but it doesn't look likely."

Tom stirs from his musical meditation. "Sure, no worries."

As you approach James you start to think you've made a mistake. This is the first time you've seen each other since the big breakup and you know in your brain, that you're still very vulnerable. Your heart, however, seems to be in control and all it's thinking of are the good times you had with James.

"Hey sexy, who were you talking to?" James asks, slipping his arm around your waist.

"A friend of Felicity's," you reply, making no move to pull away from him. You can feel his muscular arms and warm torso through the layers of fabric between you.

His closeness, his smell, the familiar feel of his body next to yours arouses you. You haven't been with anyone since you and James ended it months ago and your physical needs are starting to flood your mind.

"I am sorry you know. I never meant to hurt you. I'm an idiot," James coos into your ear, gently squeezing you closer to him. "You bring out the best in me Sophie, you always did. It was just my stupidity that pushed against that."

You don't say anything, you just try to breathe.

"I'm a self saboteur. I have my flaws, but I think I can work through them. If you'll give me a chance." He moves his mouth from your ear down to your neck and kisses you. He inhales deeply.

"I've missed you so much," he says, moving his other hand onto your belly.

You stand straight and still. You tell yourself you'll move away in a minute. Then you realise he's gently turned you to face him, your bodies pressed together all the way down.

He lifts his face away from your neck and looks at you.

"Have you missed me?" he asks, his eyes soft as though he might be close to tears.

"Of course I have," you say, your voice barely audible over the racket of the music.

"Let's go outside, I can't think in here."

He steps away from you and the loss of his body warmth crystallises in your mind what you want. You want him. You want him to be different, to be better. It wouldn't be right to punish him, he has the potential to change if he really wants to.

Just as you are walking out of the building into the cool air you hear Felicity call your name. You turn to see her chasing after you.

"What are you doing?" she says, her hand wrapped painfully around your upper arm.

"I...I don't know. I don't think we're done," you say.

"You idiot. James is ruled by his cock. He always was and always will be. Today it wants you, but tomorrow it will want someone new. He's not going to change. You don't love James Byron. You love a fantasy. Let it go and come back inside."

"I'm not really having a good time in there," you protest, looking over your shoulder to James. His back is turned and he looks like he's trying not to hear you, but he's close and it's quiet out here, you know he can.

"You don't have to stay," Felicity says. "But go home alone."

"I don't want to."

Felicity drops your arm and takes a step back. "It's your funeral. If you go home with him, we're done you and me. I'm not going to watch you throw yourself away on him." She's almost screaming, her face is flushed with anger and hurt. She walks away before you've gathered your thoughts enough to reply.

"I'm so sorry," you turn to say to James. You have to give it another go. The way you feel can't be so wrong. Felicity will come around in the end.

In the back of the taxi you and James make out all the way back to your house. You don't speak, you don't need to, he knows that you chose him and there's nothing more to say.

You make love tenderly, the way you can with a lover you truly know and afterwards you fall asleep curled in each other's arms.

In the morning you wake up to find yourself alone in the bed. You get up and walk through the house. Maybe he's just making coffee, you think.

On the kitchen table, you find a note. It's in his handwriting and is written on the back of an old takeaway receipt.

"You are beautiful, wise, gorgeous and my one true love. But I will always hurt you. I'm sorry, I was drunk. I promised you the world and all I can offer you is a world of heartbreak. J"

You're crying when you finish reading it. James has the heart of a flighty, dramatic poet and, as always, it comes with a price.

You slept with your ex, never a good idea.
You've failed, go back and try again.

C1.2 O2 You chose to walk and wait for the next one...

You look down at your ridiculous, gorgeous shoes and decide it's not worth risking your ankles just to get this tram. There's no deadline, you told Felicity you'd meet here there at about ten, and you'll still have plenty of time.

The tram just rolling away as you reach the stop. It's a little bit cold out and you wish you'd had another glass of wine before you left the house, then maybe you wouldn't mind the cool air so much. There's no one else around, and you didn't bring your headphones with you, they wouldn't have fit into your tiny going out handbag anyway. You shuffle your weight from one uncomfortable shoe to the other as you wait for the next tram.

The tram is almost empty. You take a seat towards the back and text Felicity.

"On tram now. Be there soon."

She doesn't usually respond then she's out on the town, and she's probably already at the venue getting the lay of the land and generally being seen.

You know almost nothing about this guy Eric she's obsessing over. Whenever Felicity talks about him, it's about the dreaminess of his eyes, or his hair, or whether he knows she exists. Nothing about what his hobbies are although they met through work so he must be in design somehow. She says he's blond, and tall, and the image you've built up in mind of him is more like Fabio from the cover of a romance novel than a real person. You're sure he'll be disappointing when you meet him in the flesh after all that hype.

When you arrive at the warehouse at South Wharf you immediately register how enormous it is. You could hear the music as soon as you got off the tram. There are crowds of people spilling out onto the deck over-looking the water, where unimpressed security guards try vainly to get them to stay in the designated areas.

Inside it's just as packed; several small rooms lead into one another, some with a bar, some with seating areas, and once you push your way through four such rooms you come out into a massive open hall. It seems like everyone is still in the small rooms and on the deck. The huge stage is set up at one end with a DJ trying to get the few people there to bounce, and a section in the middle which is fenced off behind white pickets that you assume is the VIP area.

People will move into the main room later when the big name performers are on, and they're drunker, for now they seem to be mingling.

The lack of bodies in the hall you feel as though the music is infinitely louder, it echoes off the metal roof and unadorned walls. You're about to turn back for another look for Felicity when you feel a tap on your shoulder.

"There you are!" Felicity exclaims. You embrace her, taking in her tasteful black jumpsuit, which covers most of her body yet still somehow manages to look risqué.

"Yeah, have you been here long? You look amazing by the way."

"It's great isn't it?" She could be referring to her outfit or to the party, you aren't sure.

"You wanna drink?" you say, hoping she'll come with you slightly further away from the brain curdling volume of the techno hall.

"Yes! Then you have to meet Eric!" Felicity is grinning, her eyes are alive with excitement and she looks a little unhinged.

"I can't wait!" you reply.

With drinks in hand, you meet Eric. He's both more and less than you expected; tall and broad-shouldered, well-muscled underneath the slim cut navy suit, but he's not nearly as macho as you expected. He is clean-shaven, and his blond hair is curly and falls over his eyes every time he moves, or talks, and sometimes even when he's still. It frames his face making him look younger and more cherubic than the Viking you might have expected.

He has a friend with him who is handsome in his own way, and a bit wolfish in the way he looks at you. While you sip your drink and try to hear what Eric's friend, Tom, is saying, you glimpse someone over his shoulder who causes your mouth to go dry; your ex James.

It's only been three months since the relationship blew up; you caught him out by showing up unexpectedly at his place and he had another woman there. He swears it was the first and only time it's happened, a moment of weakness, but you weren't fooled. It was just the first time he got caught.

Over several weeks of misery Felicity helped you come to realise that James Byron was a cheater through and through. A man ruled by his desires who couldn't say no to a friendly smile.

And now there he is, it's the first time you've seen him in person since the breakup. He's seen you too, damn it, you think.

He smiles his charming smile and your body starts to long for him even while your brain fights off the resurfacing memories.

"You still with me?" Tom asks through your fog.

"Sorry, I thought I saw someone I recognised over there."

"Did you?"

"No, I think I was mistaken." you say, determined not to engage with whatever game James is playing.

You try to get back into the swing of the conversation but you keep scanning the room for James. You're not even sure if you want to see him there or not, but you're compelled to keep looking. He's like a spider; you feel safe as long as you know where he is, but once he's out of sight he could drop on you at any moment.

"I'm sorry I'm boring you," Tom says.

"What? Oh, no I'm sorry, it's just…the person I thought I saw was my ex. There's still some bad feelings there and I keep checking to see if he's coming over, because if he is, I need to be psychologically ready, y' know?" You hope he understands, you feel like your babbling.

"I get how an old ex hovering could make you wary. Should we go for a little walk, maybe go outside for a bit?" He smiles at you and you feel a little flutter in your belly.

CHOOSE:

If you go outside with Tom, go to p 198.

If you stay here, go to p 209.

C1.2.4 O1 You chose to go outside with Tom…

"Yes, that sounds good. I don't think he'd follow me outside," you reply, smiling back at him. You feel slightly pathetic but Tom doesn't seem fussed. Take a deep breath and follow him out.

You wind your way through the closely packed bodies to the front of the building. Outside there is a small area sectioned off which seems to be for the smokers.

"You have to stay inside the ropes," one of the bulky bouncers says as Tom tries to move down the wharf.

"Right. Can we get a pass out or something?" Tom asks.

"Have you still got your stamps on?"

You look at your inner wrist and see you have a sort of circular black smudge which used to be the stamp.

"Will this do?" you ask, waving your arm in his direction.

"Yeah, I guess. If you're quick, I should remember you."

You walk away towards the docks, away from the throng and the thumping music. It's a newly gentrified area of Melbourne, and no matter how many people are supposed to live down here you always feel like it's empty.

"So, a recent breakup then?"

You blink out of your reverie and look at Tom who has been quietly walking next to you. You realise you're almost far enough from the party that you can't hear the music.

"About three months. It was a bit messy though, he–" you stop yourself, Tom doesn't need to know the details. "Suffice to say it was a bit messy and I hadn't seen him since."

"But you're still attracted to him?"

You stop walking and think about it carefully for a moment. Your heart is fluttering with the thought of James. You're going to have to detox from him at some point.

"I think I'm attracted to the idea of him, if you know what I mean, and he's not really anything like the person I have in my head." You rock back on your heels and take a breath. "He's deeply flawed and while not intentionally cruel, he does a great job of hurting people."

"Sounds tough, but you seem to have your head screwed on about it."

"The thing is it's easy to say when he's not in the immediate vicinity. If he were in line of sight, or if I smelled his cologne, it gets infinitely harder to remember he's no good."

"I had brought you out here to try to seduce you, but maybe it's not such a good idea."

"I'm sorry. I'm sure you're a lovely guy, but you're right, it's not the right time."

"Never mind." He turns and starts to walk back towards the party. There's a slump in his shoulders that wasn't there before and you feel guilty he's reeling rejected.

"You go on back inside, I'm going to stay out here for a while."

"Alright. Don't stay out too long, it's creepy out here," he says.

"I know, right? It feels much darker and lonelier than anywhere else in the city."

You let Tom walk on ahead, dawdling behind him with your thoughts.

As you approach the warehouse, you spot Jude, from work, in the roped off smokers' area. You didn't know he smoked, stopping to chat will be a way to work back up to the chaos of the party.

"Hi Jude!" You wave as you approach.

"Sophie? God, don't you look different out of your work duds!" Jude smiles back at you. You both stretch out your hands for a handshake, but you decide do go in for a hug at the last moment. His body is lean and strong, and now that you're close he smells like fruity cologne and tobacco.

"I scrub up alright," you say. "I didn't know you smoked."

"Well, I only smoke when I'm out of a weekend, I used to smoke all the time, and I've been trying to quit completely but there's something about loud music and alcohol that make it almost impossible for me to say no. I figure it's better than smoking every day."

"It's hard to give up sometimes."

"I know it! It's such a revolting habit."

You stand awkwardly side by side as he slowly drags on his cigarette.

"So, uh, how's things?" he asks.

"They're alright. Y' know, work, eat, sleep, repeat. You?"

"I'm feeling a lot better now that it's the weekend, that's for sure. I'm looking forward the DJs later on. I might even partake in some celebratory substances."

You've not heard drugs called celebratory substances before and you giggle at the odd combination of words.

"Don't tell me you disapprove Miss Faithful?" he says in a mock serious tone.

"I would never presume to tell someone how to spend their time, although I am not generally a partaker, I admit."

"You're funny. I don't usually, but I splash out on the occasional line of coke."

You and Jude keep talking long enough for him to have another cigarette and then you go back inside. You find Felicity sitting in a corner of the main room snogging Eric the Viking.

You look around and see that Tom is out in front of the DJs losing himself in the music. The dance floor is much busier now, people must like this guy better than the last guy.

Getting among the mass of sweating, heaving bodies doesn't appeal, and with Felicity otherwise occupied you wonder if you should call it a night.

You pull out your phone, seeing that it's nearly 1a.m., and text Flick.

Heading home babe, you seemed to have scored. Give me the details tomoz. X

You head out again, nodding to the bouncer as you walk out, and manage to wave down a taxi just as its dropping off a group of inebriated patrons bound for the warehouse you've just left. In under half an hour you're back at home curled up in bed.

Sophie's Path

You wake up on Sunday morning and you feel pretty good. A bit tired, and still a little sad about James, but otherwise not bad. You thank yourself for going home relatively early and roll over to grab the book you have on your bedside table.

It's a crime novel. One of your guilty pleasures is reading about psychological profilers, and medical examiners, and forensic anthropologists and how they all get themselves into the most ridiculous scrapes.

After an hour or so, you drag yourself away from the bed only to make yourself some food and coffee. Toast with peanut butter and later a banana, but it stops you being too hungry to read.

You've decided that you can afford to spend the day inside on Sunday. Your usual brunch date would be Felicity but it seems she's otherwise occupied. She hasn't contacted you yet, but you're sure when she manages to extract herself from the Viking's embrace she'll be on the phone to you immediately. Until then, all you need to do is find out whether the killer gets caught, which of course he will.

By the time you shower and change into your pyjamas ready to go back to sleep after almost a full day in bed, Felicity still hasn't been in touch. You decide to send her a message, just to tease her.

Can't believe you stood me up for our coffee date, I hope the Viking's worth it. You end it with an emoticon sticking its tongue out.

*

Max pulls you into his office on Tuesday morning for a catch up.

"I'm sorry we haven't been able to catch up as often as I would have liked since you left the team Sophie, but you know that you've been very difficult to replace."

"You're very sweet to say so," you reply.

"Sweet my shiny bald head! You know you were a great asset to this team and the only reason I let you go over to the Dark Side is because I knew you'd be a great asset to Candace too. God knows she needs some assets."

"She's not doing that badly is she?"

You know Candace has been under the pump, and had a lot of pressure coming from Aubrey to perform better but surely it's not as dire as Max seems to imply.

"She lost a half a million dollars last quarter when a client that should have been a sure thing went with another company. Aubrey was very, very unhappy with her. You wouldn't have heard anything about it though, because he expresses his disappointment in private, but the heads of department know about it. She's gotta get her team in line behind her or else they'll get someone else in to replace her."

You are silent, contemplating the stress Candace has been under and the way she's been trying to rally her team.

"She needs to start telling people how it is. Start getting people to fall in line. I know a few in the group who would work harder if they thought Candace was in trouble. They people like working for her, but maybe that's just because they think they can slack off..."

You don't realise you've spoken out loud until Max fixes you with a look. "She needs to flex a bit of muscle and trim a bit of fat otherwise she's doomed to fail."

"What can I do to help?" you ask.

"Not much you can do. Managing up is always hard. Just be yourself, maintain standards, speak up when you see someone being a jackass, let Candace know you have her back." The words sit in the air between you.

"I ran into Jude on the weekend. He was at a party I was also at." You're not sure why you mentioned it, maybe you want to gauge Max's reaction. He's a bit like a father to you and his face when you mention Jude tell you volumes. "What does that face mean?"

"Nothing. Nothing. He's a good kid, but that's just what he is, he's inexperienced and while he's not particularly young in years, he hasn't learned how to get what he wants without taking it from others."

You drop your jaw in exaggerated surprise. "I really wouldn't have picked him for a mercenary."

Max nods sagely. "I've been keeping my eye on him. Everything he does has an ulterior motive. Most of the time it's neither here nor there if he does things for selfish reasons or not, but when he threatens to put a split in the team…" He looks at his watch, "I'd better get on with things. Take care of yourself over there won't you?"

"Of course I will." You don't fully understand what he means, but give his arm a reassuring pat as you leave.

You still haven't heard back from Felicity when you get back to your desk, that's nearly three full days. It's not like her, you think.

You pick up your mobile phone and call her number. You go straight through to voicemail.

You go on to Face Book and she hasn't updated since she posted a photo of her shoes on the way to the party. You feel a cold fist start to grip your insides; an irrational crawling dread.

No, she's fine, she's just busy, you think. You try to get some work done, but the niggling feeling something's wrong won't leave you.

You find one of Felicity's emails and call her work number. It rings out and goes to voicemail. Plenty of reasons she wouldn't answer her work phone, she might be in a meeting you think as you leave her a message.

But when you put the phone down you change your mind and pick it up again. This time you dial the number for Reception.

"Good afternoon, Grimshaw Design, Natalia speaking."

"Hi Nat, it's Sophie, I was hoping to speak to Felicity if I can." You have met Nat, she's a small woman with a strong Russian accent despite having lived in Australia for most of her life.

"I'm sorry, darling, Felicity isn't here. She must be off sick or something, she hasn't been in all week."

The cold fist in your chest turns to ice, you feel sick.

"Uh, right. Sorry." Your words stumble out of your mouth as you try to keep things in perspective.

There's no use jumping to conclusions. What could possibly have happened to her? I mean really she's probably just got some bug, you think.

You keep telling yourself that all the way home, but when you get to your tram stop you stay on the tram and go to Felicity's house. She lives a couple of stops away with her brother in a group of units.

Dark is falling around you and a biting wind has picked up since you left work. It seems eerily like an omen. You try to tell yourself you're being silly, and maybe it would have worked if only one of the red flags had popped up; but with so many you're finding it harder and harder to maintain your calm.

As you walk through the overgrown grass to the front door, you can the T.V. flickering of the screen through the lace curtain. Felicity always thought that curtain was adorably kitsch.

Don't thinking of her in the past tense! You scold yourself as you ring the doorbell.

The house is red brick, you date it about 1950. There are two bedrooms, wooden floors and a massive lemon tree in the tiny backyard. You have to press the bell several times before Felix opens the door with a faraway look in his eyes.

He doesn't say anything, but you know something bad has happened.

"What is it?" you ask, barely able to speak.

Felix sighs deeply and walks back to the couch. You close the door behind you and sit down next to him.

The sound on the T.V. is turned off and the coffee table is covered in tiny pieces of paper. As he sits there Felix picks up a book, tears out a page and starts to shred it.

You put your hand on his upper arm. "Felix. What's happened?"

"No one can't find her."

You hear your heart pounding in your ears and you let your hand fall from Felix's arm.

"What does that mean?" you say.

"She didn't come home on Saturday night. She didn't come home on Sunday. Or yesterday. Or today. When she still wasn't here yesterday, and I couldn't call her, I called the police."

"Oh God." You concentrate on breathing in and out to stop yourself from fainting.

"They came over and asked a bunch of questions, but I don't know. They said they'd look for her but they haven't come back."

"Oh God," you say again. A thought flutters past your consciousness. "What about Eric?"

"Who's Eric?" he asks. He sounds like a robot. You look down at his hands and he's still tearing pieces of paper into confetti.

"Eric. The boy she's been mooning over. The one she went home with on Saturday."

"What?" Felix roars, leaping up from the couch and knocking over the coffee table. The tiny pieces of paper slide onto the floor, making a puddle.

"Eric. She went home with him. I, well, I didn't see them leave, I left early. Oh God... What if Eric's done something to her?"

You take a breath. What if she didn't leave with Eric? What if she went with someone else? What if they killed her? You might never know.

"Did the police give you someone to call?" you ask Felix, who is now pacing up and down between the couch and the upturned coffee table.

You call the number on the card Felix silently hands you.

"Have you found Eric?" you ask.

"I'm sorry. Who's Eric?" the constable asks you. She seems to be too calm. Why isn't she upset? Doesn't she know that Eric's murdered Felicity? You think frantically.

"Eric, uh, Kron I think, Felicity went home with him after the party. At least I think she did. I mean I didn't see her, but they were all over each other and I just assumed they-" You stop yourself, you can hear you're babbling.

"Take a breath, Sophie. Let me get some more information from you," the constable says calmly.

She asks you a few other questions, but your mind is numb.

Felicity's body is found under an old carpet three weeks later. She's been raped and murdered. The police arrest Eric and he confessed to accidentally strangling her in a kinky game that went wrong. He panicked and dumped her and hoped he'd get away with it.

You lost your best friend.

The End.

C1.2.4 O1 You chose to stay here with Tom…

"Oh, that's very sweet of you, but it's fine, really, we can stay here. You seem to be enjoying the music," you smile weakly. "I think I might get another drink, do you want something?"

"Yeah, a cider would be great, something dry if they have it," Tom says.

You go over to the bar. The crush of people seems to be thinning out a little but there are still a lot of people in the line for drinks.

"Hey, sexy," a familiar voice purrs in your ear.

"James," you say. You turn towards him and his scent washes over you; honey and musk and something floral. That smell meant happiness to you for so long and so recently meant only pain.

He's smiling his best winning smile at you. "I thought it was you, I saw you from way back over there and had to come say hello."

"Hello then." You try to be cool, if you are barely civil surely he'll go away sooner.

"It's been so long, don't I even get a hug?"

You know as soon as he touches you your ability to be frosty will be gone and your feelings will burst through to the surface. You hold onto your anger.

"I don't think so," you say.

"I guess not then," he says behind you, letting out an irritated sigh.

"I don't want to go around bringing up ancient history." You don't even attempt to keep the sarcasm from your voice. "But if you recall you were the one who fucked up. And you were the one who ended it, so excuse me for not being overjoyed to see you." You turn your back to him, a hot, red flush creeping up your throat.

"I said I was sorry about that, I wanted us to be friends Sophie, can't we be friends?"

"Maybe one day, but not today. Certainly not when you're three sheets to the wind, horny and lonely and whatever else."

You can smell the sickly sweet bourbon on his breath mixing with the other familiar scents. *Alcohol is part of remember?* you tell yourself, that was part of the problem.

"You're so cruel when you want to be. You don't know how you hurt me with your rejection. I wanted to be friends, to be civil, I don't want to have this awkward space between us. Can't you see that?" he says, putting his hand on your shoulder.

"You created this awkward space between us because you couldn't keep your hands or your dick to yourself. Don't make it my problem that you're feeling the consequences," you say, your voice starting to tremble. Your anger is fading and hurt is taking its place.

James is clearly not going to leave the queue so you push your way back through the crowds to where you left Felicity. You hope he isn't stupid enough to follow you.

You can't stop the couple of stray tears which leak from your eyes and trickle hotly down your cheeks and you brush them away. Felicity and Eric are busy locking lips; there is nothing keeping you here. Without another word to Tom you leave the venue, almost running, and jump into the first taxi you find as you reach the street.

You cry silently all the way home, your anger and hurt and shame all coming to overwhelm you. Once you get home, you throw off your clothes and crawl into bed, without stopping to take off your makeup or shower.

Cruelly, sleep is long in coming and your pillow is painted black with tears and mascara before your eventually drift off exhausted.

You wake up to find that James has sent you a text message. I know you still love me. I love you so much it hurts. I can be better. I'm wiser now. Don't shut me out, please. I need you. X

It takes all your willpower not to throw your phone at the wall. It's nine-thirty and you don't want to call Felicity yet. She probably went home with her Viking and you don't think it's fair to intrude on that with your bullshit ex-boyfriend baggage. She's heard enough about that already.

You turn over and try to get back to sleep but your mind is too busy; you relive all of the great sex you had with James, all the times he made you see stars you came so hard. Every time you snuck off from a party, or bailed on seeing a friend, all of the times you called in sick because you wanted to stay home and fuck. You get yourself so worked up you know you'll never get back to sleep.

It crosses you mind to call James and booty call him, but you know that would be extremely destructive. You don't operate on sexual connection alone; you'd want more and would end up getting hurt again. Instead you masturbate furiously and then take a long hot shower.

Sophie's Path

When you head out into the kitchen you remember that you don't have any food and you decide to get something from the café around the corner. They're usually busy on the weekend, but you hope they'll be able to do you a takeaway if there are no tables left.

The café owner, Brett gives you a nod when you walk up.

"How's things Sophie, my lovely?"

"Much the same, I guess. Had a bit of a big night last night so I'm hoping you can sort me out?"

"No can do in the sitting down department, my love, there's absolutely nowhere to sit. But I can do you for a takeaway, you can lurk at the front for a bit while we make your coffee?"

Almost everything Brett says is a question, he has a terrible habit of putting his voice up at the end of sentences. You always thought it was Australians who were accused of that, but Brett is English.

"I need to get some toast too. I'll get the fruit toast, I guess. You can't make the smashed avo to take away can you?"

"Sorry, love, it wouldn't survive. Fruit toast and a latte. Won't be long." He scribbles a few words on a piece of paper and weaves his way back to the kitchen.

You stand in the weak autumn sunlight in front of the café. You're leaning against the wall, your face turned up for warmth with your eyes are closed. You can almost imagine yourself slipping off to sleep in this position except for the uneven exposed brick of the wall.

"Fruit toast and latte for Sophie?" a young waitress calls. You flick open your eyes and push yourself away from the wall when a tall man in a hurry walks straight into you.

212

"Shit, shit shit!" he says, his now empty coffee cup dangles from his fingers as you gasp. He's spilled his hot long black all over your top.

The liquid cools off quickly in the autumn air and you're soon left with a clinging, cold, damp and somewhat more transparent than you would have liked T-shirt.

He is trying to pat your top dry with a tea towel which has appeared from somewhere.

"You could have burned me you know. Jeez, what were you doing?" You can't help unleashing your frustration on the poor guy, whose face is quickly turning scarlet.

"I didn't realise you were going to move. I tried to get out of the way but it was too late. I'm so, so sorry. Are you hurt? Did I burn you–" he stops midsentence, his eyes transfixed by the dark brown wet patch that is highlighting your ample cleavage.

"Hey!" You start to tell him off, but the mortified expression on his face makes you laugh.

"Oh God, I'm so sorry. I..." he says.

You dab at the stain, but it's fruitless. You're going to have to go home and change.

"Fruit toast and latte," the waitress says again, louder and more exasperated than last time.

"That's my order," you say. You move past the stranger, who is still standing in front of you awkwardly, to grab your breakfast.

"Let me buy you a coffee to make up for, uh, that," he says.

"I've already got a coffee," you say, indicating the latte in your hand. It's kind of funny how clueless and confused this poor guy seems to be. He's trying to make it up to you, but your anger at James is making you contrary.

"Right. Maybe next time." When he looks up at you and smiles you see a man who is suddenly lit up. His face, which was so plain and serious before is now glittering with life.

"I'm Sophie, by the way." You hold out your hand.

"I'm sorry, how rude of me! I'm Freddie. I'm not usually so...you know, clumsy, honestly."

"Of course you're not," you reply, before breaking into a smile. "If I can't get this top clean I'm billing you for it."

"You should, definitely." He's back to being serious, he reaches for his wallet.

"No, no, I was only-" you start to say, before he hands you his business card.

"Call me at work if you can't get that clean and I'll get you another one." When you look back at him you can see he's smiling too. Perhaps he's trying to give you an excuse to contact him.

"I have to run now. I'm really going to miss that coffee. I needed it for this afternoon. It was lovely to meet you Sophie, I'm sorry about the top, again."

"See you around," you call after him as he jogs away down the street.

You head home, smiling as you sip your latte. You throw your top into the bathroom sink as soon as you walk in the door but you don't hold high hopes for getting it back to its original colour. You may not even try, then you'd have an excuse to call Freddie.

There's something intriguing about the way his whole demeanour, his whole being, changed when he smiled for real. And he was blushing when you caught him staring at your chest.

Thankfully your thoughts over the next few days are filled with Freddie, and James's text is forgotten.

*

At work on Tuesday Candace asks to see you in her office.

"Aubrey has secured a massive contract in northern Queensland. It's for a hotel chain that's opening a new one up there. He wants someone to go up to Mackay for six months to work with them."

"Wow, sounds like a big deal," you say, not sure where the conversation is heading.

"He's asked me to recommend someone from my team, and I've put your name forward."

"Oh. Thanks." You blink heavily several times processing the information. "What does that mean?"

"Well, I think Aubrey is looking for a couple of other applicants to consider, but he knows you, your work and your background. Once he's made a decision, if it's you, you'll be given an official offer which you'll have to either accept or decline."

"Right. It sounds like a fantastic opportunity," you say, your voice flat.

You're flattered, of course, but you don't really want to work in north Queensland. You like your apartment, your friends and your parents are here. And you like being able to get good coffee on the weekends. It would be a big change.

Candace tells you a bit more about the job and by the time you leave her office you've half-convinced yourself that you actually want it.

"Have you got a minute?" you ask Max. You go straight to your old boss and mentor after you leave Candace's office. If there's anyone whose advice you value, it's Max's.

"For you, any time." He grins widely, standing up from behind his desk. "Actually, why don't you come for a little walk with me, I need a cuppa."

"Alright then."

You walk silently together to the lifts and then ride all the way down to the foyer. It seems like Max is waiting until you're out of earshot of co-workers to take up the conversation.

"So, what's up?" he says as you step into the coffee shop. There is one in the bottom of the building but Max likes to go a couple of doors up. There are a couple of tables, about half are occupied by people from the surrounding offices having meetings just like you. You sit at one of the empty tables near the window and each order a coffee.

Without going into detail you explain the offer as Candace put it to you. "But I don't know whether I want it."

"Ah," he says thoughtfully, scratching the salt and pepper beard he's been growing recently. It seems strangely lush compared with his shiny, almost hairless head. "Of course, I can't make your decisions for you, but why don't you want it?"

You're stumped. Confronted with such a simple question you ask yourself why you aren't jumping at the opportunity. Candace had said that the role came with at least two trips back to Melbourne to check in and to catch up with family. It included accommodation and living away from home expenses. The package on offer sounded fantastic, not to mention how it would look on your resume, and for your career.

"I'm scared. I don't think I'm ready. I've only been working with clients for six months, and I'd be on my own up a long way away."

"That's true. On the other hand you've been with the company five years, you know the products inside out, you're a smart and capable person. And if Candace has put you forward she thinks you can do it..."

You can feel the unspoken 'but' hanging in the air as Max stops speaking.

"But?" you say, after a lengthy pause.

"But you have to want it. Ultimately, that's what's going to make or break you up there."

You sit quietly for a while. You sip your coffee, which is too hot and too weak, and you know Max is right. He's always right.

"I know," you say finally. "I think I'm going to go for it. If it's not what I want after six months, I'll have someone else take over."

"There's the Sophie I know. Take life by the balls! You deserve to do great things, and if you're stuck here out of fear you won't do any of them."

After your coffee you head back to work. You see the business card that Freddie gave you and you put it back in your purse for later.

"I want that job," you say to Candace as you're leaving that night.

"I knew you would, you'll be great." Candace looks tired, but relieved that you'll take the offer if it's made.

She works too hard, you think to yourself as you head out of the building. You promise not to get so bogged down in work that you don't consider high-risk-high-reward opportunities that come your way.

Six months with no possibilities of bumping into James would help to heal the wound he left. You can have a fling with some beautiful blond man who can't hold down a job and possibly lives in his van. You'll have fabulous sex and nothing in common, and at the end of the six months you'll come back to Melbourne, back to your flat and your friends, and be ready to settle down. It'll be your big adventure. You've never done the backpacking thing; this might be your version.

You dig Freddie's card out of your wallet and throw it in the drawer with the rest of the networking cards you've collected over the years. If it's meant to be you'll bump into each other again, hopefully not quite so literally next time. The whole idea the universe provides is a bit much, but if he's local, chances are you'll see him around when you get back.

Aubrey is sitting in Candace's office when you come back from lunch on Friday.

"Sophie, have you got a minute?" he calls as you walk past.

"Sure."

"Close the door would you?" Candace says from behind her desk.

You take the seat next to Aubrey, your palms suddenly damp. You rub them absently on your pants.

"I know Candace has been over the Mackay job with you. I looked over your history with us, your skills, and we'd like to offer you the position. It would be effective in two weeks. What do you say?"

Fleur Blüm

You get the promotion. You don't get the
guy, by the time you get back from Mackay
Freddie's moved away and you don't cross paths
again. But then, men aren't everything.